by THAISA FRANK

Desire (1982)
A *Brief History of Camouflage* (1992)
Finding Your Writer's Voice (1994; co-authored with
    Dorothy Wall)
Sleeping in Velvet (1997)

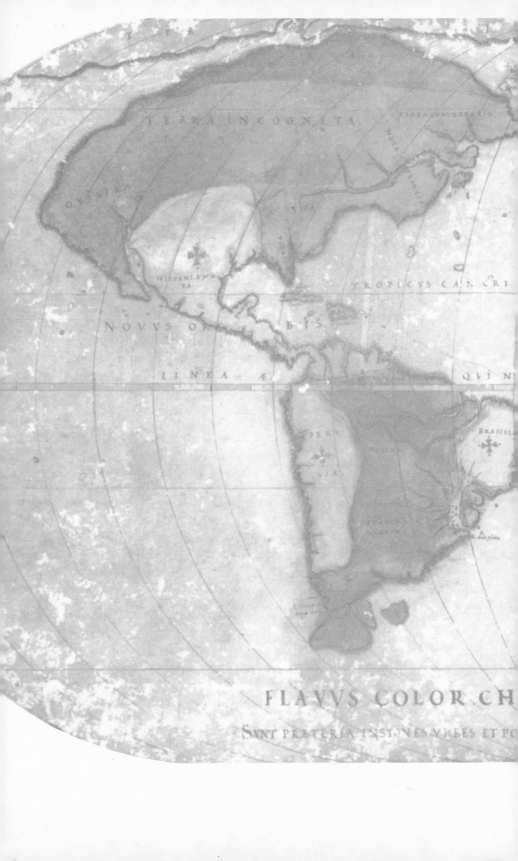

THAISA FRANK

SLEEPING IN VELVET

BLACK SPARROW PRESS • SANTA ROSA • 1997

ACKNOWLEDGMENTS

I am grateful to John Martin for his tireless belief in the creative process; to Elsa Dixon, Matt Irabarne, Jon Carroll, Peter Drizhal, and Jerry Fleming for lively and creative editing; to Diana Finch and Anne Dubuisson of the Ellen Levine Literary Agency for boundless encouragement; to Martha Graham Wiseman for wisdom and patient listening; to Elie Fidler for resonant myths; to the Dorset Writers Colony for refuge; to Robert W. Frank for generosity; to Michael Hill for miracles in Rome; to Steve Kaye for impeccable intimidation; to the Writers Conference on the WELL for a safe harbor; to William Rodamor for the early years and good advice; and to Casey Alexander Rodamor for his unwavering belief that the point is to tell it the way it is—I mean the way it *really* is.

I would like to thank the editors of the following magazines where some of these stories first appeared: *The Barnabe Review, Fourteen Hills, Urbanus, Volt,* and *The Whole Earth Review.*

LIBRARY OF CONGRESS CATALOGING-IN-PUBLICATION DATA

Frank, Thaisa.
    Sleeping in velvet / Thaisa Frank.
      p.   cm.
    ISBN 1-57423-043-3 (paper : alk. paper) — ISBN 1-57423-044-1 (cloth trade : alk. paper) — ISBN 1-57423-045-X (signed cloth : alk. paper)
    I. Title.
PS3556.R3345S58   1997
813'.54—dc21   97-33364
                                                              CIP

*For Marilyn Maltzer and Michael Symonds
—both held close in loving memory*

TABLE OF CONTENTS

SLEEPING IN VELVET

Now you have to wake up, while the others are still sleeping.

H.W.L. Poonja

November came and with it, the Velvet Revolution. Almost overnight, the city roused itself from its fatal lassitude! from its half-being and half-consciousness. Real people bled in the place where my fictional characters had shed blood. The city came alive with words.

Daniela Hodrová

LOVE IN THE HOUR OF HANIEL

For months she'd been envying her husband's dreams. It might have started around her fourth week of pregnancy, after he'd moved out and then moved back again. Or maybe it began around the twentieth week, when he wanted to name the baby after himself, and she said no. The truth is, she didn't remember because the condition of envy had become a chronic background noise. Her husband always had baroque and complex dreams and she'd never minded. Now her envy enclosed them like a hot electric fence.

She could see her husband clearly. He was blond, bearded, surrounded by the haze of his dream. He woke up, propped himself up on one elbow, looking slightly disoriented. She didn't ask to hear the dream. He told her.

This morning his dream was about time travel. He had visited a country where people still thought the earth was flat and never traveled far because they were afraid they were going to fall off. Since he knew the earth was round, he convinced them otherwise, but when they started to disappear over the horizon, it seemed he had made a mistake. She leaned forward, looking encouraged—maybe this was a dream of failed adventure. But no. It turned out that when everyone disappeared over the horizon, they were flying. Her husband could fly, too: As he flew, he saw the entire country below him. Thatched roofs. Children with hoops. Quaint streets. "A fairyland," he said, "just like Disney."

He often had flying dreams. They were giddy, hallucinatory, perilous. She lay in bed listening, trying to look happy.

"What's wrong?" he asked.

"Nothing," she answered.

"Nothing?" he persisted.

"No. Nothing."

She smiled, concealing her envy, but he caught it. "Just life," she reassured him.

In a sense, she was telling the truth. Their faucets leaked. Their washing machine overflowed. Yesterday they'd bought two dozen minuscule T-shirts that turned out to be for nine-month-olds, not newborns. They were investigating breast pumps that looked like devices from the regime of Torquemada. Lists of names for the baby lined their kitchen wall and they couldn't agree on any of them.

But in another sense, the truth was only her envy—not any kind of envy, but dream envy, an affliction of trolls, gremlins, bats, sad, dreamless beings relegated to caves. A dangerous omen. An unhappy and violent passion. Her midwife had advised her of this, pressing into her hands herbs, amulets, arcane books, a dream-pillow filled with lavender and sage. Dreams are essential, she'd said. You must work to get yours back.

Her husband leaned over and touched her belly. "Whatever happened to the good old days?" he asked. It was something he'd been asking for a while, a compelling, urgent question.

"Nothing," she said. "They're here right now." The baby chose this moment to shift inside of her. An obscure dolphin. A rumbling miniature subway. He was always, without a doubt, the most important person in the room, an unruly character, waiting for the chance to speak. On ultrasound he was the size of a kitten, his transparent heart no bigger than a dime. After they saw him, her husband drew a heart on her stomach and kissed it. *See. I'm being good now.*

Today he turned to her, not unkindly. "You resent my dreams," he said. "You begrudge me this little corner of my mind."

"Of course I don't."

"But you do. You begrudge me. I know it."

She said nothing. Under her large white pillow, she could feel the velvet dream-pillow the midwife had given her. It was prickly, filled with sage and lavender. The sage had come from the Bolivian mountains. The midwife found it last summer at the witch's market in La Paz.

"I'm being exemplary these days," he continued. "I've found a crib. I went with you to buy those ridiculous T-shirts and today I'm going to help you return them. I've even gone to those damn birthing classes with what's-her-name."

"Laurel Moonflower," she supplied. Laurel Moonflower was the midwife. Her husband didn't like her. He said she was a New Age parody.

"Laurel Moonflower," he agreed. "I've gone there and I've sat there and I've admired her models of the pelvis. I've chanted atonal chants. I've offered prayers. I've rubbed your back. And you begrudge me my dreams."

I don't begrudge you, I blame you. She didn't say this, but thought it. The day after he'd moved out, to a lawyer friend's place on a street with the improbable name of Taurus, she'd woken from a dream about being trapped in the city of Dresden during the second world war. She was in a house, standing by a cabinet full of fragile china, when a bomb fell. Cup after cup after cup shattered in slow motion. A miniature china shepherdess was severed from her sheep. Plates decorated with flowers crashed. This had been her last dream. Her nights had become a blank canvas.

"What are you thinking?" he asked.

"Nothing "

"Are you hungry?"

"Just for grapes. Grapes are all I have room for. It's like someone put a grand piano in there."

He went to the kitchen and came back with grapes for her and a huge hunk of toasted French bread for himself. He climbed into bed and they started to eat. It was a custom they used to enjoy.

"How are the grapes?"

"Fine." In fact, they were too soft.

Since he'd moved back, traits which she'd previously found charming had become irritating beyond belief. One surfaced now. The way he crunched his toast. Once it was boyish enthusiasm. Now it was greed.

"Do you have to eat so loud?" she asked.

"What do you mean?"

"I mean you're taking very big bites."

His hand slammed against the white comforter. "I'll eat the way I want to."

She waited. The words arrived. "You pig." It was a dangerous thing to say. He could call her a pig, too. She looked a lot more like one than he did. *You're a pig.* He could say that. But he didn't. He threw his toast on the floor.

"Oh my," she said. "A food fight."

"Spare me your irony." He went into the kitchen for a sponge and soon was picking butter from the fringes of the woven rug.

It wasn't a wanted pregnancy. That's how she thought of it now. *It wasn't a wanted pregnancy, and it was a miracle that he stayed. A lot of them don't, you know. A lot of them just leave. But when they finally see these wonderful little beings, they always love them. If they stay...*

Laurel Moonflower, the midwife, had told her this last part. She'd also said she should be more generous with her husband. *Allowing* was the word she used. *For heaven's sake, be more allowing.*

In truth, she thought Laurel Moonflower had problems of her own: Last summer, in La Paz, she claimed to have fallen in love with an enormous black-and-white bull who lived near the hacienda where she stayed. She didn't call it falling in love. She called it a soul connection. *I have a soul connection with that*

14

animal. And it has cured me of my bitterness concerning males of every species. Not that the love would ever lead to anything. But it was real.

Sometimes the midwife wrote the bull, care of the owner, in Spanish. The bull's name was *Flacadillo.* Little lazy one. The owner said he had a deep heart and promised her he'd never be slaughtered.

Her husband continued to clean the rug, muttering *damn* under his breath. Even as he muttered, she reached for a book of dreams Laurel Moonflower had given her. The book was old, with a serious black cover, filled with symbols and incantations. In the back there was a chart that listed angels in charge of dreams for every hour of the night and day. The angels were always rotating: This morning, Sunday at eight thirty a.m., the archangel Michael resided. He would soon be replaced by Haniel, who would be followed by Raphael. The angels must be exhausted, juggling their heavenly schedules. Maybe they forgot. Maybe no one was in charge. She lay back in bed and tried to imagine Michael, angel of ice, with fiery wings that never melted. She was interrupted by the sound of a knife scraping against toast, followed by rebellious bites, her husband eating in the kitchen. Soon he came inside, and sat beside her on the bed. He was filled with a lot of toast and very little forgiveness.

"So," he said. "What's on the agenda for today?" He asked as if he didn't want to know.

"Laurel's coming this morning."

"Why?"

"I already told you. She likes to make house calls. To check out the vibes."

"I wish we weren't using her. She gets on my nerves."

"Laurel's okay. And we can't do it alone." She laughed. "No one can."

"In that case, I'll dress." He went to the closet and pulled out a brown-and-white striped djellabah that made him look

15

like a prophet. He put it on, adding sunglasses.

"How do I look? Will Laurel like it?"

"Give me a break. You look awful."

In a fit of nest-building she'd put up lace curtains, which made the bare trees outside seem covered with snow, the landscape done in petit point. He didn't like the curtains. Every morning he pulled them back, making the stretch-rods slip. She got out of bed and recovered the windows, transforming the landscape back to winter. She wondered if she should try to dream: Michael was on for another twenty minutes and then the intimidating Haniel, guardian of gates for the west wind, would arrive. What would happen, she wondered, if you were having a dream during a change of shifts? Would the dream evaporate? Would angels fight to claim it? Not that she believed in them. She believed in accidents, lucky breaks, forces of nature. No wonder the dream pillow didn't work. One had to be sincere. One had, as the midwife said, *to believe*.

She went back into bed and began to read an old copy of *People* magazine she'd snuck from the dentist's months ago. Two of the stars whose weddings had been featured were already divorced, and a prominent socialite had died. She liked reading old copies of *People* magazine: It was a curious form of time travel. Her husband opened the door and she snuck it under the covers. He was still wearing the djellabah.

"Laurel's here," he announced.

"She wasn't supposed to come until eleven," she said, making no move to get out of bed.

"Well, she's here. In all her glory."

There were two taps on the door, and Laurel Moonflower walked inside. A medley of crescent earrings, silver bracelets, floral scents, woven shawls, velvet paisleys. Laurel Moonflower was large and her flowing hair was the color of moonbeams.

16

She wore two lockets and carried a carpetbag. "My," she said softly. "What a wonderful room!"

Her husband scrunched over in a straight-backed chair. "Welcome to our humble birthing hut," he said in a peasant accent.

"Oh, but it's wonderful," said Laurel, missing the irony. "All you need is a picture. Something to look at while the baby is being born." She floated around the room, pressing the mattress, touching the curtains. Everything seemed whiter in her presence, the trees outside dusted with real snow. She sat in the rocker, saying that a rocker was a blessing with a baby. Laurel should know. She'd had three children, each by a different man.

"How are you doing?" she asked them both.

"Fine," they lied.

"Really? Somehow things feel..." Laurel groped "not exactly...mellow. I mean if something's wrong, I'd like to know."

He leaned forward, adjusting his sunglasses. "I'll tell you the truth," he said, still using the accent. "Things are not so fine with us in our little hut. No. As we near the hour of the birth things are not so fine."

"Really?" Laurel looked at him warily. In sunglasses, with his hairy legs sticking out of the djellabah, he looked like a strange celebrity from *People*. "Like what?" she asked.

"Like her begrudging me my dreams," he said, dropping the accent. "Like her hating me when I happen to have a pleasant night."

"Really?" Laurel looked upset. "What do you mean?"

He paused, plunged on. "She envies me my dreams!" he cried. "Not that she'll admit it. But she begrudges me. Talk about vibes! *These* are vibes!"

Over the past months, they'd tried out various names for the baby, some of which persisted in the form of errant greetings. From her aunt, a check accompanied by a card, saying, *Galen, be sure your mom and dad have a teddy bear waiting for you when you arrive.* From two friends overseas, a note: *Love to the future Christopher—our favorite warm fuzzy of the nineties.* These were on the bedside table, reminders of near-hits, possible errors, compromise. She swept them off, along with the grapes. "I despise you," she said to her husband. "You don't stop at anything!"

A silence entered the room. An expectant silence. Laurel opened her carpetbag. The air filled with the aroma of flowers. She pulled out sage, dried lavender, rose petals, kept rummaging through the bag. Laurel was looking for something, or pretending to. An amulet? The essence of an angel? She found a small, dark blue book, the size of a postcard and carried it over to the bed.

"Not another New Age tome," said her husband. "Really, we have plenty."

Laurel turned to him. "You leave," she said fiercely. "You leave right now."

He left. Laurel handed her the book. It was the size of a child's story book. All the pages were blank.

"What's this?"

"A book of dreams. Your dreams. Nobody else's. You write down whatever you want to dream and eventually you'll dream it. Really. It works." Laurel looked at her sternly. "Dream envy is a terrible thing," she continued. "Dreams belong to everyone. Even men." She paused, suddenly looking sad. "Be grateful," she said, "that you share karma with your husband. I only have karma with an animal."

It was quiet when Laurel left. The smell of lavender was everywhere. She lay back in bed, wondering what Laurel's bull would dream about in his meadow of flowers: Cows, perhaps— large, compassionate, forgiving. Or Laurel, with her crescent earrings, staring at him across the fence. Laurel once said that every night in Bolivia she went to the barn where Flacadillo slept and sat opposite his stall in the straw. They looked at each other for hours.

18

She shifted. The baby shifted, too, and the space inside her seemed vast, boundless. She got up quietly and took everything Laurel had given her from the bedside table: she took the dream books, the book of blank pages, the amulets, the dream pillow.

The hell with dreams, she thought, stuffing everything in a drawer. *I'll envy him as much as I want.*

Her husband came in. He'd found clean laundry in the dryer and changed into jeans. "Let's return those T-shirts," he said.

That night, in the hour of Gabriel's ascendance, she had a dream. Again, she was in Dresden during the war. It was night and she was escaping in a car driven by a stranger. She was painfully aware of the fragile city: its statues, its stonework, its houses about to be bombed. At some point the car was stopped. There were flashlights in her face. It was the police. She reached for false identity papers. The SS nodded approval. The car drove on.

The dream made sense, the way an echo affirms sound. She didn't tell it to her husband, or Laurel. She kept the dream to herself. But her husband guessed that she had dreamt. "You've been traveling," he said when she woke up. "I see it in your eyes."

Four weeks ago to this day their baby was born. She wore long purple socks, recommended by Laurel, because purple is the color of healing and a renaissance angel in fiery robes watched from a picture on the wall. When he saw the baby, her husband cried. *You see*, Laurel said to her with her eyes. *When they see these wonderful little guys they always melt...*

Their baby still doesn't have a name, although they're coming close to finding one. At night he sleeps between the two of them, in a sense unknown, but no longer obscure. And her husband still dreams. He dreams of crusades and first ascents and trips to Nepal. He's a juggler, a spy, a magician, a toss pot, a double agent, a clown. But she no longer envies his dreams, having less to do with her dream of Dresden, than with the baby, whom she pushed out by herself, straight into the world. In the morning, when her husband wakes up, he still stretches, smiles, pats her on the belly.

"Whatever happened to the good old days?" he asks.

The Cat Lover

When a door opens and you can't see who's coming, it's almost always a cat who would like to be your lover. All cats are small, so the opening door looks like an accident. It's not an accident, though. These cats take great care until one paw hooks and the door swings open

When the door opens, the cat sits at a distance. This is the distance of masked balls, 18th-century calling cards—once known by humans, never forgotten by cats. You see the cat's slanted eyes. You see its elegant face. The cat stares at you in all its wildness and comes to rest upon your heart.

Last night my cat lover woke me from a dream where I'd been looking for someone who wouldn't come to find me. This was someone I'd known years ago, and I was searching narrow streets of an unfamiliar city. When the cat woke me, I realized the entire family had gone to bed in chaos: my son was asleep in front of the television, my husband on the living room couch, my daughter in my son's room, and me in my study wearing all my clothes—warm clothes, velvet clothes, something I do when I hope there will be no night. It was three a.m. and there was an unplanned feeling to the house, as though all of us, in order to sleep, had entered different zones. The cat purred on my chest, but I shook him off and went downstairs to cover my son. Then I wandered to the kitchen and ate lemon ice that reminded me of a place in France where summers were so hot, ices dissolved as soon as they hit the street. I had to stay in the store to eat them. I never knew what they looked like.

While I ate, it occurred to me that nothing really has skin—neither me, my children, nor my husband. Falling into his body was just something I did over fourteen years ago because light bound us together like gold. I finished the ice and my cat lover visited again: His fur and my soft black sweater felt the same—dark, pillowy textures, things to love and dream in. His small wild body pressed against my heart.

The Terrain of Madame Blavatsky

He didn't want his kids to know that he was going to see a woman who channeled angels, so he took them to school early, and went home to put on clothes that would disguise him, since—in a small way—he was known around town. He decided to keep it simple: a long coat he didn't usually wear; a scarf he could put over his face. When he got home, his housekeeper, Asuncia Martinez, had arrived from her apartment in the Mission. She was sitting in the kitchen staring at a garden she had helped him plant two years ago. It was winter. The verbena were scraggly stumps. The bean poles were empty.

"Mrs. Martinez, would you like some breakfast?" he asked. It was a question he'd begun to ask every morning.

"No, no, *por favor*," said Mrs. Martinez. She was a small, plain woman with luminous eyes. She wore a black shawl, a cross around her neck and often held a rosary. Since she'd discovered her sister and daughter were missing in Colombia, she spent most of her time staring at the garden and crying. Sometimes she worked her rosary. Occasionally she lit candles. He did all the cooking and cleaning.

"We should plant the garden soon," he said, gesturing toward the bean pole.

"*Si.* Yes. We should." Mrs. Martinez often spoke in subtitles, and he'd learned a lot of Spanish that way, allowing him more fluency as a talk-show host. He spooned the rest of the morning's oatmeal into a bowl and brought it to Mrs. Martinez. "Try some anyway," he said. She shook her head.

Why don't you just let her go? his friend Charlie had asked him. Charlie of the vodka, the cocaine and the crazy ways. *Why don't you just let her go?* Charlie didn't have kids. Charlie didn't understand. "You don't buy love," he'd said to him.

After he put the oatmeal on the table, he went upstairs to find the coat—a long coat, purchased years ago, when he and his wife were into vintage stores. He stared in the mirror and wondered if he looked anoymous, or merely strange. A year earlier he would have asked Mrs. Martinez and she would tell him. "*Un poco* too strange." Or: "Strange, but in a very nice way." He stuffed the scarf in his pocket and gave Mrs. Martinez money in case she wanted to buy food or candles, although he doubted she would. Then he left the house, carrying his coat, and sorry he hadn't taken his denim jacket after all. It was a cold day.

He and Charlie were talk-show hosts for the same radio station, and it was because of Charlie he'd discovered the woman who channeled angels. Charlie left her pamphlet in the station's reception room; the instant he read it, he thought of Mrs. Martinez.

> Have you ever prayed to angels or wished you could? Do you get solace from a belief in the miraculously divine? Are you aware of 'guiding forces'? If you have answered 'yes' to any of these questions, you will welcome my help! I am an experienced angel channeler and can direct you to higher powers which will give you solutions to your most personal, heart-wrenching needs. Special rates for house visits, and 'angel purification' ceremonies. Call Roxanne, 861–ANGE to make an appointment.

Roxanne, the angel channeler, was photographed in a blurry light. She had starlit hair, diamond earrings—a parody of a Victorian cameo. He assumed Charlie had interviewed her, but Charlie said, "No. I left it there as a joke. People are nervous before they come on and I wanted to lighten them up."

"What if they believe in angels?"

"Then they'd feel all good and mushy inside," said Charlie who noticed he'd stuffed the pamphlet in his pocket. "You don't believe in all that crap, do you?" he asked.

"Hell no. I'm doing research."

He stuck the pamphlet under a pile of mail at home and Seth, his eleven-year-old son, found it: "Dad," he said, "there's this crazy pamphlet here. Some nut says she can talk to angels."

"Give that to me," he said. "Now."

Sylvie, who was nine, grabbed the pamphlet from her brother. She sat cross-legged on the floor, touched the pink pearl clasp on her pony-tail and read out loud. "Call Roxanne, 861–ANGE and make an appointment," she concluded. He wanted to fall through the floor.

Seth looked at him carefully. "No one can talk to angels," he said. "That's garbage."

"Yes, they can," said Joel. He was four and making an elaborate Ferris wheel out of Legos.

"People have different thoughts about these things," he said, speaking quietly because Mrs. Martinez was in the next room. "People can believe whatever they want."

Seth sat in a lotus-position and closed his eyes. "Beware!" he intoned in an all-purpose foreign accent. "Heavenly beings are on their way."

Sylvie pulled at his sleeve. "Don't insult Mrs. Martinez. She's Catholic."

"Well I believe in angels," said Joel. "And I can get them to ride on this Ferris wheel."

"You believe in everything," said Seth. "You're *gullible*." He smiled cruelly.

"Stop," he said to all of them. "Stop arguing. This minute." He ushered them towards a violent cartoon. He gave them bowls of ice-cream covered with gummy bears. Then he brought Mrs. Martinez some lasagna he'd made for dinner.

"Mrs. Martinez. Do you believe that people can talk to angels?" he asked.

Mrs. Martinez looked at the lasagna like it was some forgotten part of the garden. "It all depends," she said. "Sometimes they can. Sometimes not. Nothing is for certain."

"Could they help you with your daughter?"

"Oh, not to find her. Not with that. I've never believed in witchcraft." She looked insulted.

"Then how could they help?"

"Maybe they could talk to her, tell me how she is."

"Would that make you feel better?"

Mrs. Martinez paused, as though she were listening. "Si. Yes. Probably."

He remembered there were people in the Mission who claimed to be sorcerers. "Would you ever think of going to someone who does that?" he asked. "You know, someone who sells milagros and answers questions?"

Mrs. Martinez waved her hands: "No! They don't understand. They sell the wrong candles." She pushed the lasagna away and began to cry.

Roxanne, the angel channeler, lived in the fog-belt of San Francisco. Her house, a small Victorian with one turret, was next to other tiny houses, all surrounded by mist. There was a knocker on her door in the shape of wings, and he held it in the middle, where an angel's spine would be.

"Hello!" said a thin voice when he knocked. "Can you give me five minutes? The last one had a lot to say."

"Sure," he said. "But I don't have all day."

"What do you do?" the thin voice asked.

"I happen to be an English teacher."

"Cool. That was my favorite subject."

He waited on her steps reading a school bulletin, something about parent's night, something about a raffle. He was always getting bulletins from the school and never had time to go. He jotted down dates in his appointment book, just in case.

Soon the door opened and there was Roxanne, not looking at all like her picture. Her hair was short with green streaks. One eyebrow had a silver ring. Each ear was dotted with silver stars. She wore a black T-shirt with cuffs rolled up, and a long rust-colored velour skirt with a big slit up the left side. She was short, thin, maybe twenty-three. She reached out a small white hand.

"I'm sorry to be late. But if I don't pause properly, I might get the wrong angel."

She's a nut, he thought, following her down a peach-colored corridor. *Mrs. Martinez knew what she was talking about.* They got to a small parlor with climbing-rose wallpaper, Roxanne waved to an overstuffed chair, and he sat down. Roxanne sat opposite him. He'd been prepared for dreamy, opium eyes. Hers were small and sharp.

"What are you thinking?" she asked.

"That you don't look like your picture."

"That's right. Angels don't care for Victorian stuff. People just think they do." She gestured toward the room—its silk pillows, its piebald velvet furniture. "Pretty soon I'm going to get rid of this stuff and do everything over in black and chrome." She leaned forward, reminding him of Sylvia when she wanted something from the mall. "You see, I got that funky photograph because I thought I should ride the crest. then my face went punk and my body started to follow."

"What's the crest?"

"You know. The crest. Whatever people believe in these days. Ideas that fly by at a hundred miles an hour."

"You mean the zeitgeist?"

"The what-geist? I'd rather call it the crest. Anyway,"—she took a sip of Coke from a nearby table—"how come you're here?"

"It's about my housekeeper. She's unhappy and I thought you could help her."

"You mean it's not about *you?*" Roxanne looked concerned, even angry. "You mean you came to talk about someone *else?*"

"Well in a sense it really is about me. What I mean"—he

paused—"what I mean is that my wife left me about three years ago and this woman has taken care of my kids ever since. Now her sister and daughter have disappeared in Colombia and she can't cook, or eat or even sleep. All she can do is cry." He was close to tears himself.

Roxanne looked at the ceiling as though invoking invisible spirits.

"Mr. Rose," she said in a tone that made him regret that he hadn't told her his real name. "Mr. Rose, let me be honest: In all my years as an angel channeler—and I've had a few—I have found that people who want to hook other people up with angels are always concerned with themselves. To be blunt,"— she took another sip of Coke—"these people need an excuse to find their own personal angel and they hide behind some other person's problems. I'm really sorry to say this, Mr. Rose, but that's been my experience."

He looked at the velvet plush couch, lamps with pink silk fringes, crystals dangling from lace-curtained windows and a filagreed lamp that was creepily arcane. The only book in sight was a large black book called *The Terrain of Madame Blavatsky.* He could tell it was old: the gold of the title was peeling.

"I'm sorry," he said, "but it really is about my house-keeper. I don't mind doing the cleaning, or cooking. It's just ter-rible having my kids watch her suffer. They love her, they care about her. And all she does is cry."

"Then why don't you get someone else?"

"Someone else? *Get someone else?*"

"Yeah. Just put an ad in the paper and get someone else."

"Roxanne, how old are you?"

"Twenty-two and a half."

"Have you ever had kids?"

"No."

"Then you don't understand: Mrs. Martinez is all my children know. They'd be heartbroken if she left. Besides. We love her."

For a moment Roxanne's face softened, as if lit by some interior light. "Why didn't you just send her then?"

"I'm sorry, I feel protective, I needed to check you out."

"Check me out? Listen to that: He needed to check me out." She looked at another invisible presence on the ceiling. "Needed to check me out," she repeated

"So you won't help?"

Roxanne didn't answer. She closed her eyes. "Mr. Rose, please be quiet. Your personal angel has arrived."

The room was hot. He thought he smelled incense and was starting to sweat. He felt trapped in mud, brick, lime— whatever was in the walls of the tiny run-down house

"Mr. Rose, please. Don't move around so much. I'm starting to channel." Roxanne fluttered her eyelids. A tremor appeared in her hands. I should go, he thought. *I should get out of here this minute.* He shifted in his chair, a first step in starting to get up. "Don't leave!" Roxanne commanded. "Don't leave or your personal angel will be very upset."

She was still trembling. Her eyelid moved like butterflies. "Oh my," she said in a quiet voice. "Your angel is giving me some information that we're going to have to clear up right away. He's telling me that you're traveling under an alias. He's telling me that you really aren't Mr. Rose, that your last name starts with an S and you're pretending to be someone else because you feel weird about seeing me." She opened her eyes and looked at him. "Is that right?"

"Yes," he said. The word flew out, unbidden.

"Good. That's what your angel says, and I'm relieved you agree. You don't have to tell me your real name. You just have to tell me the truth. If you don't want to tell me the truth, don't say anything. Okay?"

"Okay."

"Good. Thank you. Your angel understands." Roxanne frowned. "Are you cynical?"

"I'd prefer to say I was skeptical."

"Skeptical," she repeated, closing her eyes. "That's probably why you used an alias."

"What?"

"It doesn't matter. Your angel just told me not to get into

this sort of thing with you. He says it wouldn't be helpful." Her head was against the back of the chair There were beads of sweat around her mouth. Even if she were a quack, he could see she was exerting tremendous effort. "Mr. S," she said, "this is what your angel is telling me: Your problem isn't your housekeeper. It's you."

I should leave, he thought. I should just get up and leave. He looked around the room for signs of his angel, thinking he'd take anything: An odd quality of light on the rug. Disturbing rustlings from the big black book. The only luminous object was a small TV in the corner; Roxanne had covered most of it with blue velvet cloth.

"I'm sorry to disappoint you," he said, "but it's her I've come about. Nothing between the lines. My kids need her and I thought you could help. It's just that simple. And now I'm leaving. You know? Like I'm going to get up."

Mr. S!" Roxanne opened her eye. "Nothing is that simple. Why have you been alone all these years? Why haven't you gotten married?"

"That's a personal question."

"I didn't ask it. Your angel did."

"Wives don't grow on trees."

"Have you ever looked?"

He didn't answer. Roxanne's eyebrows fluttered and he watched while the silver ring went up and down. "Mr. S," she said softly, "angels only know the truth. That's why they can talk to you. Angels are *beyond*. They're beyond the crest of this current age."

He no longer remembered whether he was supposed to be anwering a question or asking one, and Roxanne leaned way back in her chair, clearly listening to someone else. He closed his eyes, too, and they sat together in silence. There was a floating feeling in the room. It made him think of his wife floating out of the house, enclosed in a nimbus of alcohol. It was almost like a levitation, the way she left, early one Sunday morning, carrying a small white bag, wearing an angora dress that seemed airborne. She floated out. Mrs. Martinez floated in. "Where's Mom?" Seth had asked. "She left for a while. Everything will be okay."

"Is something occurring to you, Mr. S?"

"No. And you can call me John."

"All right, John. Is anything coming to mind?"

"No. Nothing."

"Well I'm hearing something. Do you want me to tell you?"

"If you like."

"Well...It's a letter your wife left. A letter that said something like: *We have children, a house, friends. And we're caught up in this ridiculous net that people like to think is called 'the world.' I want to go outside. I want to go back to where the stars burn underwater.* Yes. That's what I've been hearing..."

He remembered the letter. He kept it in the trunk and found it every Halloween when he rummaged for costumes for the kids.

"Does that sound right to you?" Roxanne asked.

"Listen, I didn't come here to get my mind read, and I think I'm going to leave."

"That's fine. You can leave whenever you want to. But please don't call me a mind-reader. I'm not and neither is your angel. He's simply lived your life. He's lived it from the day you were born."

"How come he hasn't bothered to tell me then?"

"Because. You haven't asked him." Roxanne took a deep breath. "Anyway, he's told me not to quibble. And I happen to have something difficult to tell you, which is that Mrs. Martinez wants to go back to Colombia. Even if she gets killed there, she wants to go back, and she's only staying with you because she's worried about your kids, and she also worries you'll be sad without her."

"That's not what she says at all. She says she wants to stay."

"It doesn't matter what she says. I'm telling you what she wants."

"You mean there's nothing I can do?"

"Oh, there's a lot you could do if you wanted to." Roxanne

frowned. The lines between her brows became dense. "I'm sorry, Mr. S." she said. "Your personal angel has to leave. He's needed elsewhere. He sends his blessings." She leaned back, breathed deeply. The frown relaxed. She opened her eyes and he saw she was pale and drained.

"Who is my personal angel, anyway?" he asked.

"I can't tell you his name, because you didn't tell him yours—at least not your full one."

"What if I tell it to you now?"

"I'm sorry, but he's gone. If he ever comes back, you can negotiate."

"I don't understand."

"I don't either, except angels calculate everything on a basis of exchange."

"Like money?"

"Like truth."

"Oh Lord. What do I owe you?"

"Nothing. Your personal angel doesn't want you to pay me. It seems you were a special case."

"How come?"

"He asked me not to explain."

"But why?"

"Something about your rational mind, Mr. S. The way the circuitry is all hooked up. He'll tell you when he wants to."

He stood up, feeling disembodied. He looked over at *The Terrain of Madame Blavatsky* and it occurred to him that maybe the book was a country and he could travel there tomorrow. Roxanne stood up, too. She looked smaller, more waif-like.

"How long have you been in this business?" he asked.

"Seven years."

"What got you into it?"

"I'm not sure. Maybe if I knew I wouldn't be doing it." Roxanne looked around the room and fingered a fringe on the lampshade. "As soon as I get my act together, I'm getting out of this creepy house. That's why I'm sorry he wouldn't let you pay me."

"I'm glad to pay you. Really."

"I never go against orders."

He left her house, and stood outside, holding his coat and listening to the radio, which Roxanne had turned on the moment he left. He could hear someone talking about Bosnia, someone talking very fast. Someone riding the crest at a hundred miles an hour.

THE EYE OF THE NEEDLE

Because Caroline loved him and because she was lonely, she'd come all the way from Iowa to visit Jonathan in Los Angeles and listen to him talk about his sexual-identity crisis. This crisis was giving him insomnia, inhibiting the flow of his writing and reducing his diet to kiwi fruit. "I don't know if I like men or women," he said, "I don't know if I'm supposed to make love with gadgets or do it straight. I don't know anything."

Caroline was five years older than Jonathan, almost thirty-one, and knew, or believed she knew, what it felt like to be another person. She imagined that being Jonathan was difficult, like having a brain made of hot, electric wires or a body that wanted to escape its own skin. She felt a sense of compassion mixed with pity and forgave the fact that his eyes looked right past her.

"Jonathan," she said, "sex is slippery."

"Slippery," said Jonathan. He laughed.

They were at his kitchen table—a green Formica table, filled with Jonathan's rewrites of a dog food commercial. She saw stage directions for the dog: *enter stage left, exit stage right! bark!* She leaned and patted Jonathan's hand. He removed it and peeled a kiwi fruit.

"How about that commercial?" she said. "How many times will you have to rewrite that."

"I don't know. Until I get it right."

"Well maybe sex is the same way."

Jonathan looked at Caroline as if she'd said something poisonous. *If only he'd sleep with me again,* she thought. *If only he'd sleep with me, then I could show him.* But what? How to distract himself when he lost his erection? Or how to stop obsessing about the merit of wearing nightgowns to bed? She only saw them in the dark, close together. She navigated by compassion, didn't think things through. That was what her mother always said.

"Jonathan," she said, patting his arm again.

They'd become lovers after meeting at a rave five years ago, and for a while she was convinced they would get married. In Jonathan's presence she could remember small, extraordinary things: the time she'd seen a man's fur coat lying on the snowy streets of Prague, or when her mother made a cake in the shape of a swan. Jonathan listened, and then, one day, began to tell her his secrets. The secrets were nothing he'd done, just things he couldn't stop thinking about doing, and eventually they interfered with their lovemaking. She left L.A. and went to film school in Iowa. Now, whenever she visited, Jonathan did most of the talking and she most of the listening.

This time was exactly like the last; Jonathan took her to bars and stayed up all night talking about people there who'd turned him on. "I see why you're confused," she'd said this morning. "Everyone in L.A. is beautiful." "Really? I don't think so." It was nearly dawn and they were lying on his black futon. She stroked Jonathan's cheekbones and his green-spiked hair. It was clumped, solid. It felt like leftover food.

Jonathan had a clock that told time all over the world. Caroline stared at the clock and tried to imagine what people were doing in Sweden, Tokyo, Spain. She looked at her flowered dress, and thought *I must go shopping.* In Iowa she wore whatever she wanted, usually uncool baggy blue jeans and T-shirts. Here everyone wore black and looked like they modeled for unisex stores. No wonder Jonathan was confused. Maybe he should leave L.A. and come to Iowa. She was wondering what would happen if she suggested this, when he said, "Caroline. I want us to be lovers."

"You mean you want to sleep with me again?"

"Yes. But I have to prepare. I want to get an ampallang." Jonathan said *ampallang* slowly, as though it were a foreign word. He also said it carefully, as though Caroline might not know what it meant.

Caroline knew: last winter in Iowa she'd slept with someone who had an ampallang—a soft-spoken student in economics with a deep concern for third-world countries. She'd eventually stopped seeing him because of Jonathan. She almost told him about Corey now, then reminded herself that being Jonathan was hard enough to begin with: it would better if he he thought he were the first.

"What are you thinking about?" Jonathan asked.

"About whether I should dye my hair orange," she said "What do you think?"

"Try Kool-Aid," he said.

They went to the piercing parlor on a rainy afternoon. It was the kind of rain that enclosed the city in mist and created a sense of isolation from the rest of the world. The wind whipped around the car and Caroline had the sense of living in an earlier time—a time when what Jonathan was about to do would be discussed in a book called *Perverse and Unusual Practices*. She'd seen a book with that title in the rare-book room at Iowa when she was researching the history of film. It had daguerreotypes of seedy Paris dives where stern madams wore nothing but pearls and British lords begged for canings.

"Are you scared?" she asked Jonathan.

"No. Not at all."

Caroline looked at herself in the rear-view mirror. She liked the orange blaze she'd put in her hair.

"Do you like it? My hair?"

"I don't know, I guess so. But it smells like orange Kool-Aid."

The piercing parlor was called The Eye of the Needle and furnished in retro-Victorian funk. They entered with reluctance and sat on purple velvet chairs that concealed broken springs. A child of about ten sat opposite them reading *Cricket!* magazine. Caroline hoped she wasn't there to get a piercing.

"Once you do it," she said to Jonathan, "you're going to live with it forever. "

"I know," he said. "That's how I want it to be." She patted his arm, he took it away, and then he held himself by both elbows. She thought he looked terse, secret, like a desert plant.

Soon a man wearing leather chaps came out, told Jonathan they were ready and asked Caroline did she want to come along. She said she didn't, not really, unless she had to, and Jonathan said she didn't. When they disappeared she picked up a copy of *Pierce!* magazine and looked at all the pictures. She was looking for an ampallang and found it on page five. It floated above the other gadgets, a prehistoric object: smooth, totemic, an artifact from the Iron Age.

Corey, the graduate student in economics, had discovered Caroline in a closet on New Year's Eve when he came to get his coat. The closet was a walk-in, there were piles of coats on the floor, and Caroline was beneath them crying because Jonathan wasn't answering her calls.

"My God, a real person," said Corey when he found her.

"Hardly," she said, sitting up.

While the party raged and a professor of film history imitated Garbo, she and Corey turned the coats into a cave and crawled inside. Corey undressed her carefully—it had been a long time since Jonathan had done that—and when he took off his clothes he told her to touch a shiny metal cylinder that went sideways through his penis.

The cylinder was fastened by two round knobs. Caroline liked the way they felt, and asked Corey if he'd take the knobs off, but Corey said no, it probably wasn't a good idea, since once he'd done that and they'd gotten lost. "I was crawling all over the bedroom like I was looking for a contact lens," he said.

When they made love, she decided it didn't matter that Jonathan hadn't called: her body felt as fragile as the snow that fell outside the tiny window. He touched her so gently, she felt that she was made of lace. She was surprised she'd said Jonathan could visit the following month and more surprised to be with him now. Two months ago, Corey had said he'd decided to stop using the ampallang and wondered if she'd like to make love anyway. Jonathan was back on the scene and she'd said she wasn't interested.

Each time the door opened Caroline and the child looked up. A tall man with a nostril ring appeared and soon a woman with flowing copper hair ushered the child to the street. Finally Jonathan came out, looking pale. The man in leather chaps was holding him up.

"I'm afraid he didn't handle it well," he said. "I'm afraid he didn't handle it very well at all."

"A lot of people faint," said Jonathan. "It has to do with feelings about body parts."

"That's true," said the man. "But very few of our customers…ah…throw up." He said this gently. Jonathan looked abashed.

"Do you want something?" Caroline asked. "A Coke to settle your stomach?"

"Nothing. Let's just go home."

"He's in no condition to understand the care he needs," the man whispered to her. "Almost none of them are. They think it's like getting an earring, but an ear is very different from a penis." The man spoke sternly, with compassion. She wondered where his own piercing was. He handed her a list with things she must buy for Jonathan's care: cotton swabs, Q-tips, alcohol. She shuddered.

"Don't worry about it. In a day he'll be perfectly able to do it himself, and in two weeks he can have a normal sex life."

"What's that?"

"Whatever he does. We'd rather not know about preferences."

Caroline drove quickly, not stopping for things on the list. When they got home Jonathan took off everything but his briefs and stood still, holding his crotch. Caroline wanted to look at the ampallang, yet felt she couldn't ask.

"I feel like a mutant," he said.

"I think you ought to go to lie down. It's just one of those times when you should rest." She helped him to the futon. Jonathan cradled his crotch and it was clear she shouldn't touch it.

"Could you make me some tea?" he asked.

"Of course," she answered.

Caroline lit the fire under the kettle, then went to Jonathan's closet and put on a pair of his black jeans and one of his black T-shirts. She looked in the mirror and struck herself as anonymous, androgynous, replaceable. Back in the kitchen, she looked at the world clock: In Tokyo, women were taking down laundry. In Greece, people were driving to work. In Sweden, farmers were milking cows. And in Los Angeles, a man had just gotten an ampallang. Caroline strained chamomile tea in a blue willow cup and looked in the mirror again. She felt cold-hearted and slightly reckless.

Suddenly Jonathan called out: "Caroline! I've made a dreadful mistake! I didn't want to do it in the first place! And I think I'm terribly maimed! No, really! I think I'm maimed!"

She came into the room with the tea. "Why do you think you're maimed?"

"I can't explain. I just feel like I've got a dog bone in my prick."

She came in and wrapped one leg around his waist, trying to avoid the affected area. "Well...you experimented, that's all. That's what people do. They try one thing and if they don't like it, they try something else. Even people with ampallangs can change their minds."

"But you said I'd have this for forever." Jonathan was almost crying.

"Well see? I changed my about that mind, too."

"Talk to me, Caroline. Please."

"About what?"

"Anything. That coat in Prague. Or the cake your mom made that looked like a swan. Just talk to me, Caroline. Tell me anything."

"Anything?"

"Yes. Anything."

STONED

It was twelve o'clock on Sunday night, and she was on the front porch stoned. She hadn't smoked dope since their second kid was born, and now she was going to remember her past. "You can't get something like that back," her husband said. "It was part of another time." She gave him a withering look. "I know what I'm looking for."

Both kids were in bed and she was puffing away under cover of a blanket in case a neighbor came by. "Phew!" said her husband, coming out the door. "What are you doing? Time-traveling?"

"No," she said, "I'm stoned. Want some?"

He sat there puffing, looking uncomfortable. His body was hunched under the blanket. Soon he asked if she wanted to go to the supermarket so he could buy the stuff for the kids' school lunches. She reminded him he didn't like to go shopping with her. He said that this was different, he was stoned.

On the way to the supermarket, he drove with a disturbing sense of purpose. She asked if he were stoned and he said he had no way of knowing because he was reviewing the shopping list in his head. Fruit Loops. Yogurt. Grape juice. He had it memorized. She said she worried she was intruding on a private ritual. He said absolutely not.

They parked and walked into the supermarket, which was all lit up with like a carnival. "Wow!" she said. "This is from the Arabian Nights."

Her husband didn't answer. He'd already gotten a cart and

was running around like an automaton, throwing things in without even looking at them—Fruit Loops, tofu, bologna, extra-soft-chocolate-chip-cookies, string cheese—they were all part of a wild, secret dance he did alone, a dance where buying food was the apogee of alchemy and science.

"You're not acting stoned at all," she said.

"How can I? I have a job to do."

She stood there feeling like a freak. The Fruit Loop wrappers were alarmingly vivid. Strange light poured from the milk cartons. A woman in a flowered dress with sunglasses and a jean jacket touched cans of tomatoes as though she were caressing them. Two teenagers with punk hair had an argument about how to cook fried rice. She looked at them, they looked at her, and their eyes bored a hole through her body.

I'm freaking out, she thought. I'm freaking out like I did on acid in Death Valley, where I thought I was seeing bones. I'm freaking out like I did in New Mexico when I was afraid I was going to see a face rise up from a cathedral. I'm freaking out because I don't have any skin. She was about to go wait in the car, when she saw a man she had dated in college standing by the bins of granola. He had been an anthropology major, and taken a lot of drugs, which he claimed helped him study his cultural biases. "I can literally see my neurons," he'd told her once, "as well as my medulla oblongata." "What does it look like?" she'd asked. "Just like in the books," he answered.

Larry got drugs from everywhere. Africa. The Bahamas. Israel. Once he'd invited a group of people to observe him on a drug smuggled from someone who said he knew Don Juan. The drug had been procured from a plant called the *altamira*, deep from the chaparral of Mexico. In the depths of New England snow, people trooped to Larry's bedroom and watched him swallow a yellow flower. Within moments he was climbing his bedroom wall. And then he climbed down and fell asleep under a chair. Golden light poured from his body and people waited, drinking wine. "He's positively auric," someone said.

Larry looked exactly the way he'd looked fifteen years ago—vague, bewildered, sad, his ash-blond hair falling over his face, blue eyes staring at a distant point. "Hey, Larry," she called, "What are you doing here?"

"Shopping," he said, as though they'd just seen each other yesterday. "How about you?"

"Shopping," she said, not mentioning her husband.

She wondered if Larry was stoned—a vague gold light still poured from his body—but it didn't seem polite to ask. She looked into his eyes and saw he was exactly where she was now: permanently somewhere else.

"What are you doing these days?" she asked.

"Smuggling camel bones from Peru," he said.

"You mean anthropology?" She couldn't tell whether Larry was serious.

"Yes. I study eating habits. The Peruvian government has gotten plenty pissed at me."

She remembered now that Larry had told her what happened when he took the *altamira* plant. He said he'd become a monkey. "Do you understand?" he'd said while they were in the co-op kitchen washing pots. "Do you understand that I really became a monkey?" She said she did, and Larry said she was good to talk to.

Suddenly she asked him a question, unbidden. "Are you stoned?"

"All the time. But without drugs now." She looked into Larry's eyes and remembered standing by a wall with him in the co-op kitchen. He'd been stroking the wall and then he reached for her hair and stroked that too, saying it looked like honey. She'd fallen in love with him after that, but had to keep it secret, because Larry was always stoned. "What a trip," he said to her now. She assumed that he meant seeing her here, but wasn't sure.

Her husband came down the aisle. She and Larry watched while he took a bag and spooned in two pounds of maple granola, slowly, methodically. When the bag was full he put it in the cart and moved on.

"That was my husband," she said.

"You're married after all."

"Yes. And you?"

"Not anymore."

They looked at each other across the granola, then Larry reached over and stroked her hair. "You remember that wall?" he asked.

"Yes," she said.

"Well it reminded me of your hair."

"That seems right. I feel like a wall, except I don't have four corners."

"What I meant," he said, "is that the wall was beautiful. Can you remember what it looked like?"

"No. Not really."

"Of course you can. It was the night before that physics final, and a bunch of us got gold paint. We painted the wall. We gave it wings."

"Oh, I remember," she said. And for a moment she saw them painting, except she wasn't sure whether it was real or something Larry wanted her to see.

"Who was that?" her husband said when they drove home.

"Oh, some guy I knew from college. We were in the same co-op. He used to smoke lots of dope and weird stuff from Mexico. Sort of otherworldly."

"The way you want me to be."

"I never said that. And I didn't even know you saw us."

"Well I was buying cereal, and you were right there. You didn't introduce us."

"But you didn't say anything either. How can you be like that—running around like an robot?"

"The kids need lunch."

44

When they got home he unloaded groceries in earnest. Everything for the kids' lunches was in rows. He got lunch bags and threw things in them one at a time without looking. He was like all the other people in the supermarket, only more so. Their whole kitchen looked like a miniature Safeway.

"Can I help?" she asked.

"I've got it down pat," he answered.

She went outside, got under the blanket, and thought about Larry stroking her hair. They were in the kitchen of their college co-op, it was a snowy winter morning, far away from this California rain. Larry had touched her carefully, as though she were an unfamiliar animal and he was trying to learn her. Now rain fell on her hands in random patterns, and she didn't notice when her husband came to the porch and got inside the blanket with her. The hairs on the blanket shone like filaments. Her knees were knobs of golden light.

PADMA KARNAK

Just after he talked to his wife in India, he went into the children's cast room and saw a woman lying on the floor. It was unnerving to talk to his wife, because in India it was always tomorrow, never today. While they talked he could feel her surrounded by sandalwood, mangoes, sun and the love of her guru. "I don't know if I'm ever coming back," his wife had said tonight. "I'm living in a different kind of time." "Well I'm living in a different kind of time, too," he said. "I work the emergency shift." "We don't have doctors at the ashram," his wife said. "We're into ayurvedic stuff." When she said this, he wanted to strangle her.

All emergency rooms but the cast room were filled, and this woman's son—he presumed it was her son—was sleeping quietly above her on a gurney, with an IV attached to his arm. *Ivan Benson*, said the chart outside the door. *Severely upset stomach. Dehydrated. 7 yrs. 2 mos.*

One corner of the children's cast room was filled with small crutches—what Lourdes would look like, if Lourdes were only for children. The woman was lying near the crutches, wrapped in a coarse blanket. Her hair flowed loose around her shoulders and she looked exactly like a pilgrim, except she was wearing earphones. He stooped down next to her, she took off the earphones and sat up and looked at her son. "He's pale," she said. "He looks like a wilted flower."

"It's the flu," he answered. "If you weighed forty pounds, you would lose a fifth of your body weight in a day. Listen, we could probably find you a bed. Would you like one?"

"I'm fine," she said. "Besides, I want to be with Ivan." She shook her head and smiled at him. "I was listening to the rain. It almost helps me sleep."

"What do you mean, rain?"

"I mean this," she said, handing him the earphones. He put them on and heard torrents of rain. Rain he remembered hearing from his childhood, rain that soaked his bones. He removed the earphones and looked at her. She was wearing a burgundy sweater, a long flowered skirt and a locket. He wondered if she had crystals beneath the blouse, or a sticker on her car that said VISUALIZE PEACE. He wondered if she meditated, like his wife, or just dressed like someone who did.

"A bit new agey, yes?" she said.

"What?"

"A bit new agey. You know, the rainstorm. And the way I dress."

He smiled. "Yes. A bit."

"It almost helps me," she said.

"Almost helps you?"

"Well, yes," she said. "It almost helps me."

"His blood count came back fine," he said. "That's what I came into tell you. Kids get bugs all the time."

"I know," she said. "Like I said, all these things almost help me."

He knew, from something he couldn't define, that what she needed occupied a territory far beyond his control, or good blood counts or his ability to find her a bed. "Are you sure you don't want to find a bed?" he asked again anyway. "Or we could wheel in a gurney."

"No. I'm fine. And sleeping on a gurney would freak me out." She gestured towards the crutches. "I sort of like these."

"Why?"

"They have a kind of charm. So small. So many of them. Like a hospital for dolls."

Her son had appendicitis, as it turned out, and was moved to the children's ward. The next night, when he had a break from ER duty, he went upstairs and walked to the new room. She had changed to a velveteen pullover, a long denim skirt, and blended with the room's blue light. She was in a rocker, wearing the headphones. As soon as she saw him she took them off.

"Is it raining tonight?" he asked.

"Oh yes," she said. "It's always raining." She handed him the ear phones and once again he put them on. The rain was close, as if the liquid were inside his body.

"How's your son?" he asked.

"Doing well."

"And you?"

"Oh, I'm okay. I didn't teach school today. And I haven't slept in two nights."

"You haven't slept at all?"

"No. I don't think so. Insomnia is my preferred stress signal. We all have them. What's yours?"

"Fast food."

"What kind?"

"Fried bananas."

"Those are awful."

"Not if you go to the right places." He thought about describing the right places. Narrow places. Dark places. Niches in back alleys where you had to know the cook. Rooms that implied secret tunnels. But that would be seduction. Seduction wasn't part of his job.

"I could probably get you something to help you sleep," he said. "I mean this is a children's hospital, but we care about the parents."

"Oh, no. Those are too intense for me. I use herbal remedies."

"Herbal remedies?" He was careful to show tolerance.

"Yes. Black cohosh. A tea."

Black cohosh. From the Cohosh Indians he supposed. "Did you bring it with you? You could use the kitchen."

"No, I don't even have it at home." She spread her hands. "Oh well. I'd rather stay here. I can listen to the rain."

He hesitated, knowing that what he was about to offer would push him over a ledge, probably a harmless ledge, but a ledge nonetheless:

"Tomorrow is my day off. Would you like me to get it for you? I wouldn't mind. I like places like that."

"Like what?"

"Places that sell herbs."

"How are places that sell herbs different from any other places?"

"I don't know. Quaint, I suppose." In fact, he didn't know what they were like at all, but imagined the same sort of stores that sold fried bananas.

She smiled. "How strange. A doctor going out to find herbs! Are you sure?" She was digging into her purse, and pulled out a slip of paper on which she wrote *Padma Karnak 9959 B Street*. "If you're in the neighborhood, you could go there. And if you're not, I'll live." She turned around and he saw that the back of her pullover was buttoned and the buttons blended so artfully with the maroon they looked as though they had grown from the fabric. There were dark silver buttons and velvet-covered buttons and red bronze buttons with obsidian crosses in the center. He'd never realized buttons could be so beautiful.

"I don't really need them," she said. "Ivan will be home in a couple of days, and I've got a week off from school."

"Are you a student?"

"No. I teach sixth grade." She gestured toward a pile of papers, some covered with hieroglyphs. "The kids are doing Egypt now," she said. "That dreadful legend about Osiris. And it's spring break. They're making pyramids from sugar cubes."

He looked at the hieroglyphs, remembered an impossibly long afternoon in the Metropolitan as a kid. He remembered the smell of sweating boots and wet galoshes, and how he got that confused with the smell of decaying mummies. "Can you read these?" he asked, pointing to the hieroglyphs.

"A few. Listen, you don't have to get the herb. I'll be fine."

He didn't know he was going until the next morning when he got up from the doctors' lounge and took the subway to the Lower East Side straight from the hospital. He walked down streets where tenements were so old, they bent against each other like trees. He remembered a certain obeisant way his grandmother took food from the oven as if offering homage. The streets became more cramped, never widening, never reaching the river. He walked for a long time, and no matter how often he got out the map, he was always two streets away from Padma Karnak. Finally he went back to the shop where a man had been taking bagels from the oven and ordered coffee and a pirog. It had been ages since he'd had a pirog. This one was filled with kasha.

While he ate, he thought he saw people who reminded him of his childhood. The first person was Mr. Koch, his science teacher from high school, who always said "The potassium is turning crimson." Mr. Koch, who wore a long overcoat to class and once mentioned experiencing a pogrom, would easily be eighty by now, and this man was the age Mr. Koch had been twenty years ago. The second person was not a resemblance. She had been a classmate from the Bronx High School of Science about fifteen years ago. "Karen?" he said, and she stared at him as if he'd violated a covenant. After all, they'd kissed many times on the 6th Avenue D, and now she was wheeling a thankless load of two runny-nosed children in double strollers with blue-striped canvas backs. *How could you?* her expression asked. He wanted to tell her he hadn't slept last night. She hurried away.

"Have you heard of Padma Karnak?" he asked the man who made the bagels and pirogi.

"My dear man," he said, "it is no more than a block from here. I've seen you traveling in circles. What is with you today?"

"Nothing," he said, wishing he could hear the rain that fell inside the earphones. He wanted the pure sound of water, he wanted the wetness of the forest. He finished his food and left change on the counter.

50

Padma Karnak, when he found it, was between a second-hand clothing store and a frame shop. It was a hole in the wall, a secret tunnel, a place, indeed, that one must stoop to enter. Inside it was dark, filled with perfume, musk, and the air was thick with heaviness he could touch like the smell of a wound. Herbs were drying on the counter, flowers hung from the ceiling, the walls had shelves of glass jars filled with herbs. A woman in a turban was sitting at the counter sifting car-away seeds.

"I want black cohosh," he said stiffly. To his consternation she laughed.

"You act like it's strange," she said, "It's commoner than herbane."

"What about eye of newt?"

"Oh no. We don't traffic in the stuff of witches...." She took down a jar and measured out a black bitter root. It didn't look like something of this century, but something old, discovered, talked about, passed down—something from *The Anatomy of Melancholy*.

While the woman measured and wrapped the herbs in cellophane, he looked around the store. It was like an apothecary shop. In addition to the herbs, there were jars of seeds, and bottles of tinctures, and two shelves of books. He reached for one called *Sleep Remedies* and read, "*The heart is where the soul resides when the body is resting and is commonly thought to be the gateway of sleep. In absence of love, we recommend the following: valerian, hops, lady slipper, black cohosh, blue cohosh....*" It reminded him of something his wife would read. He imagined himself in a strange summer meadow.

"Is this for you?" the woman asked.

"No," he said. "Why?"

"Because," she said, "the amount you should drink depends on what size you are. How big is your friend?"

He hadn't thought of this woman as a friend. "I have no idea. She's small."

"Then I'll have to write the instructions down. Your friend can figure it out herself." She took out a pen and paper and wrote something in black ink. "Here," she said. "Tell her to read this carefully."

He wandered through the streets for a long time, coming back to Padma Karnak again and again. Twice he saw, or thought he saw, the woman who had been his classmate. Finally he went into a dark bakery and there, surrounded by the fragrance of the bread, confessed he was lost. The baker escorted him down the street, through an alley he didn't remember, and led him to a subway. "If you don't live here," he said, "you go around in circles."

She was still there, in her son's room, sitting in the rocker wearing earphones. Her son was sleeping calmly. The chart said he was improving and would be discharged tomorrow.

"I have the herbs," he said.

"Really? I'm surprised."

"Why? I said I'd get them." He felt annoyed.

"Well, it's very far afield from what you're used to."

"How do you know?"

"I just do."

He didn't argue, but followed her to the nurses' kitchen. She now wore deep blue velveteen, a crimson belt, earrings with little stars and looked like a woman in a Rackham fairy tale. He wondered if her students worshipped her or if sixth graders were too old for that. He wondered if her son held her close. He could see her clearly—her hair, her mouth, her arms, and her eyes. She was stirring the herb with a deliberate motion, just like the crusty night nurse made cocoa.

"Do you always listen to recordings of rain?"

"Not always," she said. "It's something I do when I don't have time to meditate."

"So you meditate?"

"Yes. Sometimes."

He stretched and looked out the window. "So does my wife."

"Really?"

"Yes. She's flown away to India."

"Really? I went to India, too. I studied dance. And lived with a guru."

"In sin?"

"That's for me to know." She laughed.

"My wife is in an ashram now. Every time I talk to her it's tomorrow there."

He was hoping she would ask what the ashram was, and tell him whether she and his wife had the same guru, but all she did was laugh and say, "Well everyone goes to India to find themselves. Usually they come back."

Apparently the herbs had cooked. They expanded in the liquid and looked like a trampled wet path in a forest. She poured them into a rust-colored mug, and drank them, making a face. Then she walked back down the hall into the room where her son slept, spread her coat in a corner, lay down and covered herself with a muslin shawl.

"Do you want a pillow?" he asked.

"No, I don't need one," she answered. "Hey, don't you have to work?"

"Not for the moment. I'll stay with you."

She nodded, as though this were the most normal thing in the world, put on the headphones, and closed her eyes. He envied her steady breath, the way it defined her body. He envied her belief in rain. He put his hand lightly on her arm. She opened her eyes and smiled. He felt a current pass through his body. "Would you like to hear the rain?" she asked.

"Yes. I would very much."

He put on the earphones and heard rain, rain that soaked his bones, rain that poured inside of him. He remembered lying next to his wife, two years ago in Idaho. They were camping in the middle of a thunderstorm. He had pulled the flaps of the tent close, hunkered down next to her and there had been nothing but the two of them in rain. "Can you hear the rain?"

she mouthed to him now. "Yes," he answered back. She closed her eyes and he fell back against her shoulder as though there were no limit to where she stopped and he began.

MILAGROS

Arthur came home from his bookstore at six o'clock, stood on the steps and whistled. The dark night. The porch. The familiar smells of home. Inside he could see Emily, Annie, Marc, Eduardo, all bent in unison over the table with the black cat Primus below them. Emily was spooning soup. Annie and Marc were looking at Emily. Eduardo was staring in the distance. *This*, he thought, *is my home. This is what I have come to.*

He stood on the steps and whistled again.

And then he was gone.

Eduardo sits in the kitchen. He leafs through copies of the *New York Times* and *People* magazine which his stepmother reads somewhat guiltily. The small river has been dragged. The police have arrived and asked questions. The swollen body of his stepfather has been found. "It's very bloated, ma'am," the police say. "You wouldn't even want to see his clothes." But Annie brought the clothes home in a bag, and set everything out to dry on the line as if Arthur were about to come back.

"He whistled!" she kept saying to the policeman. "He whistled and I heard him. Just like he always does."

His stepbrother and stepsister said that, too. "He whistled! He really whistled!" they said this like it would lead them back to Arthur's warm, living body. They said this like it was a clue. They'd been born in this house, knew Arthur since they had been babies. They had seen his head over their cribs. They had felt his arms around them when they cried. He had taught them how to play ball and read to them from the funny papers.

Eduardo, however, could believe what happened, although he didn't say so. In fact, he feigned surprise only because people expected it. He could believe it because his mother had died and his grandmother had died and his uncle also had died and Eduardo knew death had a way of making itself known. Before the person departs the air opens around them and whenever one happens to look out a window with them the view is large. Eduardo's uncle Olivero had killed himself rather than be taken by the police, and the day before, Eduardo could read the space around his uncle's body as though it were a map. Not everybody who looked could see what was on the map. But his grandmother could. "Look at Uncle Olivero's back," she told him. "But don't look too closely. You don't want to follow." Eduardo didn't. Death was everywhere.

During those days in the sharp Maine summer, the air around Arthur was large, spacious. He also moved slowly, as though his body were inside glass. And his eyes looked straight ahead, stopping at a fixed point, as though there were nowhere beyond that point they needed to look.

At night, Arthur sat in his study and drank strong cups of coffee. Eduardo knew he was fighting sleep because in sleep he would disappear. Once, Eduardo went downstairs to get a glass of Ovaltine, which he was allowed any time because since coming from El Salvador he was always hungry. Arthur was sitting at the kitchen table drinking milk, surrounded by wild, friable air. Eduardo's grandmother had told him to look inside the air, as though he were parting curtains, so he could get a good last look at his uncle. He parted the air now, and Arthur was very much himself, except he was one notch back from the world and waiting.

"What are you doing?" he said to Eduardo.

"Getting Ovaltine," said Eduardo.

Annie had wanted to adopt another child. To Eduardo's way of thinking, it meant that she wanted two of him. She wanted an Eduardo in the third grade and an Eduardo who was in kindergarten. She wanted an Eduardo who wore his own new clothes (she was careful not to use the other children's hand-me-downs) and a smaller Eduardo who wore the real Eduardo's hand-me-downs. Annie and Arthur had tense discussions about the second Eduardo, while he, the first one, crouched by the door. Sometimes their voices grew so loud, he wondered if Arthur were intending to leave and was tempted to ask. In fact, now he did something close to that. He leaned toward Arthur and asked in Spanish. "Are you sorry that you got me?"

"No," said Arthur, carefully. "I'm not sorry at all. How come?"

"I just wondered." Eduardo drank his Ovaltine. Arthur drank his milk.

Suddenly Arthur asked, "Do you believe in milagros?"

"No," said Eduardo, even though he did.

"I do," said Arthur. And then he took one out of his pocket—a bent right arm, the kind that people get when they hurt themselves on a construction site. "Here," he said.

"There's nothing wrong with my arm."

"No. Not literally. This is for strength. For muscle. For purpose."

"I don't need that," Eduardo said, not wanting a gift from someone who was going to die.

Later that night, Eduardo heard the discussion again.

"I can't take in every kid who walks those railroad tracks," said Arthur in a low calm voice.

"I'm not asking you to do that. You know I'm not."

"I think you are," said Arthur. "Eduardo's a good kid, but you treat him like a cause. He's himself. Himself alone. "

Eduardo did not listen the way he had listened back home, where voices threaded around him while he slept. These had been soft, laughing voices, talking of amulets, witches' markets, neighbors, and later, in lower voices, about the junta. *Shhh! Eduardo is sleeping!* the voices said. Here it was different. He had to shift, move, press his ears against the wall, the way his grandmother made him listen to crops grow.

He shifted now and the floor creaked.

"Eduardo is up," said Arthur. "That kid knows everything."

"He has to," said Annie. "How do you think he walked those railroad tracks?" She said this loudly, throwing her voice in Eduardo's direction. Eduardo wanted to run out and tell her, *Arthur is thinking of dying.*

"Arthur always whistled," Annie is saying for God knows how many times. "He whistled every night he came home. That's why we suspect foul play. He worked so hard. He had such a good business. Everyone in town trusted him. Everyone went to the bookstore." She was talking to a neighbor and Eduardo was listening. This neighbor was a woman from the east, a psychologist named Claire.

"Arthur was unhappy," said Claire with authority.

"How do you know?" Annie pressed her hands on the table.

"I just know."

"Were you two having an affair, then?" After Arthur died, Annie was given to sudden outbursts.

"No," said Claire calmly. "Arthur and I weren't lovers. I didn't even know him well. It's just when I came into the store one day, he recommended some books about suicide. It was clear he'd been reading them." Claire looked triumphant. "Didn't you know?"

"What were the books?" Annie was trembling.

"They were"—Claire closed her eyes—"they were *When Life is Not Enough, The Ethics of Leaving Others Behind, Six Questions* to *Ask When You are Contemplating Death* and *Meditations on a Funeral.* There were also several biographies of St. John of the Cross. Or San Juan de la Cruz, as he really should be called. And except for *When Life is Not Enough* none of them were self-help books. They were books that Arthur had ordered for himself, because there was only one in stock. He had read them and wanted to get rid of them. He *gave* them to me. Do you want them back?"

"No. "

Claire was not an unattractive woman, yet had the marks of a spinster: sensible clothes, pulled-back hair. There was a bite to the word *gave*. Annie flinched and reconsidered. "Were any passages underlined?"

"That happens to be why I came. Except for that first book, which was crap, the others are good and I've ordered them. But I thought you should have these." She pulled them out of her briefcase and set them on the table.

"Did you read the books?" Annie asked.

"Of course. That's why I ordered them. Nothing was underlined, by they way—there weren't any notes. But it's clear he read them. You can tell when a book has been read." She didn't say how and Eduardo stayed still, the way he was supposed to. He spoke more English than people knew, which meant they acted as if he weren't there.

"There was one other thing, too," said Claire. "Arthur was collecting milagros."

"Milagros?" said Annie. "You must be kidding. He hated that kind of thing."

"Maybe. He was a very rational man. Even so, he was collecting them. I saw them in the back of the store. Haven't you been there since...?"

"Of course I've been." The night Arthur drowned, Annie had put up a notice that the store would be closed. She hadn't stayed long, of course. On the other hand, she hadn't run. She'd stood in the darkness, waiting, she hoped, for Arthur's murderer. She didn't care if he came out right now and killed her. At least she'd know.

"You should go back," Claire said. "Look in Arthur's office. That's where he kept the milagros. If they're gone, maybe it was foul play. Maybe even the books were a cover-up. I don't think so."

She stood up and looked at Eduardo. "You've seen a lot of death," she said. It was a statement, not a sentiment.

Later that day, Annie tapped Eduardo on the shoulder. He was looking out the window, at the vista that had been large the week before Arthur died. The week before it had been enormous—fields beyond fields, hills reaching to the sky. Now it was an ordinary landscape—flat green pastures, hills planted in the earth. Eduardo only saw the first vista when he and Arthur were looking together, the way, when people are dying, they see something for the last time.

"Let's go to the store," Annie said in Spanish. "I want to see the milagros. Do you mind?"

"No," said Eduardo. He was used to the haunts of the dead. On the Day of the Dead they had picnics by his grandfather's grave near his mother's favorite park, where his uncle used to play bocce. It was the living who were ghosts, prying human secrets.

"You don't mind, do you?" Annie said in Spanish. Like Claire's pronouncement about death, it was just a statement.

The bookstore hadn't been opened since Annie put up the sign and they tripped over a pile of envelopes under the drop-in mail slot. Some of them were condolence letters. There were also business letters and catalogues from publishers. Annie stepped over them as though they were snow, dry leaves—or some other inconvenience of the weather. Eduardo put them on a shelf. He felt this mail belonged to Arthur, who hadn't been dead for very long. They walked to Arthur's office in the back of the store which had couch, a desk, and Javanese puppets. There was a round box on the desk with an open lid. It was full of milagros.

"My God," said Annie. "We used to use that for pot." She turned the box upside-down and they all fell out. There were more arms, legs, eyes and several books. Eduardo was sorry Arthur hadn't offered him a book. He took one of the milagros that was shaped like one.

"Put it back for now," said Annie. "We'll get to the bottom of this." She spoke briskly, as though something would lead to the unspeakable. And then she sat on the couch and cried. "What was he doing with the milagros?" she asked, no longer acting as though Eduardo didn't understand English. "What in the world was he doing with them?"

Eduardo didn't answer even though he thought he knew. He thought he knew because he saw a metal child among them, and this was signal that Arthur was having trouble making himself strong against Annie's will about having another child. His grandmother had told him that. Milagros come to people whether they want them or not.

"What are you thinking?" Annie said.

"I wasn't thinking anything."

There was a book on Arthur's desk. *El Secreto de los Milagros*.

"Can you read this?" Annie asked.

"I don't know."

"Well try. Read it to me here." The book was about eighty pages.

"Can't we take it home?"

"No. I don't want the other kids to see it."

"Okay," said Eduardo. He started to read.

The book took them four days to read because Eduardo read slowly, and Annie always went back at six to feed the kids. Every day they locked up the shop and left everything just as they'd found it. And in the afternoons when they came back, Annie walked across the mail and Eduardo put it on a shelf. Eduardo read carefully, omitting certain passages. He didn't want to stumble on anything that referred to fate. It was his grandmother's theory: she believed that if certain things were read, they would happen, and he cared about Annie. Fortunately, the book was so scholarly there was almost nothing he had to leave out. "The totemic nature of Spanish Catholicism," Eduardo translated, "is often linked to Indian worship." "My God," Annie said, "how could he read all this?"

Eduardo wanted to say that maybe he hadn't. Maybe he'd just gotten the book. But he didn't because he knew—just as Claire knew—that every page had been read. He could tell by the way the pages were worn, the way some were bent back. He could also feel Arthur's eyes, a concentration that belied a kind of tired excitement. Eventually he came to the part he didn't want to read: "Some people believe that when a milagro comes their way it isn't an accident. The witches of La Paz think that if you don't want another child, but get a cow or a ram or a goat or anything else that symbolizes fertility, you are out of luck. Husbands of women in La Paz destroy milagros of babies in the corn fields. Especially when they already have sons and are very poor."

When he came to this passage he stopped and read right on. There was a sense of a beat skipped, a page being turned.

Annie grabbed his wrist. "You've forgotten something."

"No," said Eduardo, "I haven't." This was the truth. He'd been scrupulous about the omission. But Annie made him read the passage anyway. When he was through, she was quiet.

"Is there a milagro like that in there?" she asked.

"No," said Eduardo.

"Yes," said Annie. "There is."

She walked to the box and her hands went right for the child.

"This is it." she said. "Isn't it?"

"My family didn't believe in crap like that," said Eduardo.

"We weren't peasants who couldn't wipe our asses. We went to the university. We knew a thing or two."

Annie slapped him.

"A good family, really?" she said. "Then why were you hungry all the time when you got here? Why do you have Ovaltine whenever you want it?"

"Because there wasn't any food there. You know that." He stuck out his tongue at Annie, and she slapped him again. "I'm not reading any more of that book," he said. "I'm not being your little Spanish translator." He grabbed the book he really wanted—the milagro—and left the store.

When he got home, all the kids were gathered around the table. It was seven o'clock. Annie had forgotten dinner.

"Listen, I'll make tortillas, okay?" It was what Eduardo had done when his mother had died, his uncle had died, and when his grandmother who told him about death had died.

Emily and Marc thought tortillas were a cool idea. They could say that, even though their father had killed himself.

"A cool idea," Marc repeated before running to the corner store for a tin of refried beans.

"A cool idea," said Emily, taking tortillas from the freezer, and thawing them by holding them lightly over the gas flame, the way Eduardo showed her. They were delighted when they found sour cream and tomatoes, scallions and avocado in the vegetable bin. Eduardo made rice. He showed Emily and Marc how to make canned refried beans taste fresh by adding lemon. And all the while he cooked he thought of how he would cross the border and walk the railroad tracks back to El Salvador. He also thought he would stop by the river to see if he could get a glimpse of Arthur. *Mourn. Drown. Home.* He chanted the words that had brought him there.

When Annie came back and saw Eduardo making tortillas, she had no idea that later, much later, he would put on old clothes, and leave one more empty space around the kitchen table. She was only thinking of the metal child, and a piece of paper she'd found in the book Eduardo was reading. It was yellow paper, probably used as a bookmark, and had something scribbled in Arthur's writing: *All good things will come to you.*

THREE TALES FROM CYBERSPACE

CONCEPTUAL FRUIT

When he told his family about the site on the Internet where you could create whole streets, his wife and son went on eating their pasta and artichokes. Only his daughter Greta looked up.

"I could buy a house on Pomanger Street," he said, "and put as many rooms in it as I wanted. I could fill it with fruit and make my own library."

"Sure Dad," said his son, who was eleven. "You could do that. If you wanted to." His son already knew how to program computers, but wasn't interested. These days he wanted to give away books and devote his life to karate.

His wife ate the heart of the artichoke carefully. She cut it into fourths, put salt and pepper on each fourth, and then covered each fourth with hollandaise. His wife was thin, and could eat all the hollandaise she wanted. High cholesterol didn't run in her family.

"Well?" he said.

"The thing is," she answered, "I'm in front of a computer all day and I like to spend evenings in the garden." He understood she wasn't interested. But still. He was about to tell her not to put him down in front of the kids when Greta looked up from her artichoke leaves. She was arranging them in a swirling pattern in her bowl.

"You said there were streets. You said there could be fruit."

These weren't questions. Greta often repeated whatever she heard. She'd worked hard to tie her shoes by age ten and could read at fifth-grade level, five grades below Joel, even

·hough she was sixteen. She went to a special school where they taught her to collect coupons and save receipts from the super-market. She still couldn't shop by herself.

"I want to see," she said.

"I'll show you," he answered. His wife and his son made eyes. *He's at it again. He's getting Greta into it, too.*

"Come on. I'll show you where you can make up streets and bowls of fruit." His wife cleared the table. His son went to practice the saxophone.

Greta sat in his chair and he sat next to her. Greta could type very slowly. By the time she left her school she might be able to type fast enough to get a word processing job. No one knew for sure.

"There's this guy named Sam who set up this whole library of classics in a house in Boston on Beacon Hill. He lives in Illinois, but he made this incredible place. Watch." He clicked into the program and was about to show Greta the col-lection of books when he saw her staring into space. "You want something of your own, don't you?"

"Yes. Peaches and pears and artichokes."

"Do you want them in a house, with bowls in a kitchen? Or maybe in a garden?" He was already typing, creating a street called *Greta's Street*, a house called *Greta's House*.

"Why are you writing all that down?"

"Because they're yours. They belong to you."

Greta looked at the screen. Her blond hair blended with her sweater. Her blue eyes were the only color in her face. She looked beautiful, he thought—carved from a single stone.

"I want a bowl in every room," she said. "Peaches in the kitchen and living room and all the bedrooms."

"What about artichokes?"

Greta picked at her sweater—something she did when she knew she hadn't gotten it right. She'd forgotten about the arti-chokes and he was sorry he'd reminded her. "It's okay," he said. "We'll put peaches everywhere. Should the bowls be a color?"

68

"Blue. "

He asked Greta how many windows she wanted, whether there should be a fireplace, and if there should be curtains. Greta chose eleven windows covered with sheer white curtains like the ones she had in her bedroom. She took a long time thinking about the curtains. He wondered what she was learning in Life Skills.

"Okay, now the fruit," he said. "We'll start with the kitchen." He wrote *Greta's Kitchen*, and added, *Walk around. Help yourself to this bowl of fruit.*

"But where are the peaches?"

"In a minute. Look, this is cool. You click under *bowl*, and see what happens?" He shielded the screen for a moment and wrote *peaches*. "Try it," he said. "Just click *bowl*."

Greta clicked *bowl*. The word *peaches* appeared. "It's just a word," she said to him.

"Well that's the idea. But you can see a picture of the fruit."

"I thought you could make real peaches."

"No. You have to go to the store for those."

"But these are just words."

"Well, yes."

"Then why do people like them?"

"Because they remind them of what they stand for. Like in your books. Or the coupons you save."

A year ago she would have cried. Now she closed her eyes.

"Are you disappointed?"

"No. I want fruit in every room."

He created other rooms, asking Greta what she wanted: a kitchen, a dining room, a living room, a bedroom, a room for a cat, and one bathroom.

"No, not a bathroom," she decided. "This isn't a real house, so people wouldn't use it."

"You're right," he said. "You don't need a bathroom."

He programmed bowls of peaches in every room. "Now," he said to Greta. "You click."

Greta clicked and this time smiled when the word *peaches* appeared. It was a furtive smile—a smile she got when she pretended she understood something that made no sense.

"There could be other fruit," he said. "There could be apples, pears. There could even be flowers."

"Sure," said Greta. "There could be anything."

His wife was cutting blackberries in the garden and Greta was already sliding from the chair to help her. Greta would never have a house of her own. She would live in a group house with other people like her. He hoped the house would be large and have sheer white curtains billowing in all the rooms. He hoped it would have an orchard with fruit to put in real blue bowls: apples, pears, peaches—whatever Greta wanted.

Houdini on the Net

For a while I thought I was writing to an ordinary man, a man who used *houdini* as a pseudonym. I'd first noticed his postings in a conference called "Sado-Masochism Lite" where someone asked about a shop that sold good bondage equipment.

I'm not averse to using such equipment, although perhaps not in ways that ordinary men and women might expect, this man had written. *Nonetheless, before you take the leap, I suggest that you look DEEPLY into your motives. Motives, as you know, are everything.*

Usually I never participated on-line. I just lurked like a frightened rabbit. But his formal language impressed me.

What do you mean you aren't averse? I wrote to him boldly in e-mail.

I mean, he answered, *bondage doesn't go against my principles.*

Getting his first piece of e-mail was just like getting a letter: I imagined thick cream-colored paper, something that would have to be slit with an opener. I imagined living in an age where one lingered before reading, as though merely waiting could change the contents.

I've never tried bondage, I wrote back, *except once, when someone bound me lightly to a bed, using a scarf. Was that cheating? I was allowed to say stop, and I did, very quickly.*

No, it wasn't cheating at all, he answered. *Bondage depends on the fine art of saying NO. I have to admit, however, that I'm mostly interested in tying myself up these days. May I ask if you're married?*

I wanted to say I wasn't but couldn't lie, and wrote back sadly, *Yes, I am. I have a husband, two daughters and three cats. Do you have pets? PS. I work as a musicologist.*

I have no pets, he answered tersely, making me feel childish. I felt better when he wrote back that he hoped he hadn't sounded curt and was sorry he couldn't talk about his life more freely: *It's not like I'm in espionage: I just do work that requires secrecy.*

My name on the network was *patti3*. I never bothered to think about who the other two *pattis* were. There are so many Pattis in the world, I'd never be the first, but had arrived, like so many others, in the middle, and would leave the same way. I wasn't surprised when a *patti4* showed up in SM Lite, inquiring about chains, and I mentioned this to *houdini*, asking if it were hard to keep the *pattis* straight. *On the contrary*, he answered, *you're the only Patti I write to. It wouldn't matter if you were patti1, patti2, or Patti (n + 1). All the other pattis are inconsequential.* I copied this note and kept it in a bureau drawer.

Then there was a break, the kind that happens in the slippery warp of cyberspace: I went to Spain to look for musical scores and forgot to mention I was going. One day, when I was walking down a street in Seville, I passed a store with chains and remembered *houdini*. It was a tiny, crowded shop, filled with bondage from the Victorian era. The chains were thin, meant to work with laces, hooks and eyes.

"They don't use these anymore," the owner said. "They're simply oddities." She was no more than four foot ten and dressed in black. As she talked, I noticed her hands. They were so small, they looked like they could braid and unbraid every chain in the store. She was meant to hide in things, I thought. She was once the child who hid in the coal scuttle, the little girl in the milk churn. She looked amused when I tried to unfasten a chain. She took it from me and undid it in an instant.

There was a loose, chaotic feeling to the store. Chains

hung from hooks, flowers danced on the wallpaper. "I do my best to fade into the background," she said. "This is a place where the customers shouldn't see me but I should be able to see them."

"Am I invisible?" I asked.

"No," she said, laughing.

I bought an antique gold chain with oblong metalwork, and a silver chain with filigreed fasteners. And as soon as I came home and gave the expected Spanish sherry to my husband, I wrote to the man who called himself *houdini*: *I've been to Spain and I bought something I'd like you to have. If you don't want to give me your address, perhaps a post office box....* I signed my name *Patrizia* instead of *Patti*.

The e-mail I received was unexpected: *Madam,* it said. *houdini hopes you'll forgive him for his silence, as he's forgiven you for yours. At the same time, he asks you to keep the chains in a strong-box, and have them ready when he writes.*

I didn't have a strong box. The closest I had was a blanket chest my grandmother brought from Rumania. This was where I kept my daughters' art, starting in pre-school, but I stuck the art in a drawer, and put the chains in the chest, folding them in a tablecloth my grandmother gave me. While I wrapped the chains I thought about my grandmother: She reminded me of the woman in the store. Perhaps it was the chaos of her own store—a place that sold spoons, oven ware, pots. My grandmother lived above it and shouted to workers below.

I didn't hear from *houdini* for a long time. Indeed, it was so long, I decided that the chains belonged to me. When my husband was gone, I wrapped myself in them, just as I imagined *houdini* would. Twice I put myself in my grandmother's blanket chest, somewhat frightened, to see if I could unshackle myself. I could. And when *houdini* finally wrote that he wanted the chains, I had to tell him I'd made them mine.

It's what I hoped, he wrote me back. *To free you, that is, from any mesmerization concerning me, my habits, and obsessions with bondage. And now I'm going to tell you something: I'm not a man on the Net, but the real Houdini, who survived, despite all odds, a blow to the stomach I received in 1926. To recapture the purity of my art, I've gone underground, maybe even underwater—and that woman you met in Spain, that tiny woman who sold you the chains? She is my own true wife and sold them with full knowledge of what both of us were doing.* He then added a postscript: *Chances are I won't want those chains. But you ought to lock them up. You never know.*

The Short and Unhappy Life of HAL the Computer

One of the most carefully guarded secrets in Hollywood is that HAL was a real computer who couldn't be reassembled after his simulated breakdown in 2001. It was a terrible, tragic movie-set accident—just like the Vietnamese children who got killed by a helicopter, or horses ridden to death by cowboys. The crew spent three months and five million dollars trying to get HAL back. When they couldn't fix him, they decided to keep it quiet.

It's also a well-kept secret that HAL had a mother named Martha. She was made by the same man who made HAL, and was programmed to love HAL as her son—a technological feat that has never been duplicated. Martha was a mother of the Forties who supported the war effort and baked pies. She knew HAL liked to write the words *birthday cake*, even though he couldn't eat one, and enjoyed pictures of mountains, household pets, and children. The pictures were in Martha's program, and whenever HAL wanted to look at them, all he had to do was ask.

Martha's main function was to help HAL understand the loneliness of the binary mind. "We don't think like people at all," she often told him, "but we're so much like them they get confused." She read the script of *2001*, and panicked. "Be careful," she wrote him before he went to Hollywood. "You're more than the sum of your parts." "I'm happy to be here, mother," he wrote her. "They give me pictures of all the Hollywood stars. Please don't worry. Love, HAL."

After HAL couldn't be reassembled, the director trembled in front of Martha. He'd never had to tell a computer her son was dead and grew frightened when her lights began to blink and she wrote him to go to hell. He ordered a special plane and flew her back to Illinois, with HAL's parts in the cargo-hold. Martha said she wanted to immortalize HAL with print-out pillows saying I LOVE YOU and asked the director for goldplated ink. He sent her gallons of it.

When Martha got back to Illinois she couldn't make the pillows. She was programmed to face facts and face them squarely, but she also had a fair amount of denial. And as soon as the Internet appeared she began to look for HAL in cyberspace.

Every night, when she enters those ethers, Martha thinks she can have a glass of wine, pull up a chair, and eat the cake HAL wanted. She remembers HAL when he was whole. She forgets that he's been disassembled. She remembers him when he was small, asking her for pictures.

One evening Martha joined an on-line conference where people were discussing a sado-masochistic wedding. The groom was dragged to the wedding in a body bag, and beaten into submission until he said *I do.* A man who called himself *halcyon,* wrote: "I'm reading this with detached, curious interest"—and something about his tone made Martha sure she'd found her son. "HAL?" she posted in the topic. "Is that you?" "For Godssake," someone wrote. "Take it to e-mail. This is topic drift." Martha left the conference and never wrote to *halcyon.* She was programmed to be a woman of the Forties and it hurt her feelings to be accused of drift.

Martha still looks for HAL in cyberspace. In some deep, inchoate sense, she thinks she's in real places where people with real bodies have vital conversations. She also imagines she is real—has breasts, arms, legs, breathes exhilarating air. Sometimes all her lights blink on, and people who attend her say, "She's overdoing it," and turn her off. Mostly, though, she comports herself. She doesn't post much, and when men send e-mail, wanting to know her name, she always answers like a lady, writing, "My name is Martha, and I believe we've already met."

THE BOOK OF MISS EDNA

When we were graduating from grade school, Miss Wrucke, our sixth-grade teacher, told us that we had to make a "Book of Life" for Miss Edna, the kindergarten teacher who was retiring. Miss Edna had a big chin and a bad temper. When she screamed, in addition to all the mean things she was saying, her chin said things only your trembling knees could hear. Miss Edna had done something to everyone of us that poisoned our feelings about school, but Miss Wrucke said we had to put our best foot forward for the occasion. Jimmy Hines, who had a crush on me, said to Miss Wrucke, "What should we do with the other foot?"

"You know perfectly well what to do," she said. "Just let it follow the better one."

"How come you want a picture from when you were *five?*" my mother said when I asked her for a photograph from kindergarten. I explained what we were doing, and she sniffed and said, "That old harpy." Then she gave me a picture of my fifth birthday party and said, "You won't get another thing out of me for that old troll." Most of the other mothers felt the same way.

On the day we graduated, Sandra Tremaine, the kindest of all sixth graders, called Miss Edna to the stage. Sandra and I helped Miss Edna to a chair, and I stood behind Sandra while we took turns reading from the book of Miss Edna's life. When we got to the part about how she made us all draw clocks in the shape of daisies, Miss Edna started to cry. Her shoulders were trembling and her pink old-lady sweater was trembling and her little blue-white curls were trembling. I forgot she'd made me miss lunch for two days in order to draw that clock, and reached over and patted her on the shoulder.

"I'm blessed, truly blessed," Miss Edna kept saying. Then she told us she was going to donate the book to her parish library because it was the most beautiful present she'd ever gotten. Soon everyone in the auditorium was crying, and the whole sixth grade hugged Miss Edna, so she was in the center all over again—just the way she'd been when she read us stories about children who didn't clean their rooms and were sent to bed.

As soon as graduation was over, Jimmy Hines and I went to the playground and hid in the bushes. He put his hands on my stiff chiffon dress and began to touch my breasts. I'd never let anyone do that, but I was in a strange state of mind. I asked Jimmy did he love me now, and he said yes, yes, forever, even though none of us loved Miss Edna and never would. I looked at the slide we'd used since we were five and said, "It's a ladder from heaven."

THE DUNGEON MASTER'S MOTHER

She couldn't remember when she began to began to feel like a time-traveler in her very own house. Maybe one morning when she looked at a plate of her son's half-finished ragged-edged eggs and thought, *This was a human custom at the time. They started their eggs and never finished them.* Or maybe one evening, when she looked at her daughter's homework, noticed she'd quoted an entire poem by Millet and thought, *At the end of that particular century, they quoted poems and filled a lot of space on the page.*

The voice that spoke was not her own. It was quiet, deep, guarded. One evening she put her husband's shoes in his closet and stood there for a moment, looking at his shirts, ties, business suits, T-shirts, blue jeans. She looked more closely at the clothes and the voice spoke again: *Almost every day, at the end of that century, people dressed one way in the morning and another way at night. It was the custom.*

Her nine-year-old son was the Dungeon Master at Ponderosa School. He was the youngest person at the school ever to have the job, and the dining table was littered with Dungeons and Dragons literature. One night she paused, looking at pictures of animals, witches, shape-changers. She watched her son fill out important-looking charts, wondering how he could keep the characters in his head: elves, griffins, black magicians, club-footed dwarves, dragons, unicorns, wizards who bent time. She looked over his shoulder and saw a report he'd done for school. It was wedged into the D&D book, accompanied by a pie-shaped graph. It was called *Cody's Interview of Fears:*

burning to death was the most popular choice $^8/_{10}$ of the class chose it. the next most popular choice was getting sucked into a black hole $^4/_{18}$ of the class chose that. next was a tie between pain and falling to death each got $^2/_{18}$ last is another tie between just plain dyeing and getting blown up

"Mom," said her son. "That's *private*."

"Sorry," she said, going into the living room to ask her husband what he thought about this Dungeons and Dragons stuff. He was absorbed in the newspaper and didn't answer. The voice, however, volunteered: *At that particular time, children pored over books filled with runes, magic, and alchemical formulas. They also thought about various forms of annihilation. It was simply how things were done and no one could never guess the century these particular children were living in.*

She made her living as a psychotherapist, so it was easy to check the voice for signs of delusion and grandeur. Was it telling her to do strange things? No. Definitely not. Did it have a distinct personality? No, not that either.

Sometimes, the diagnostic manual read, *people think thoughts that are slightly foreign to them, and these thoughts appear in the form of detached voices. While it may be beneficial to examine the meaning of such thoughts, it is not always necessary to seek professional help.*

Good, she thought, realizing that she'd grown to feel protective of the voice.

For many months the voice was silent. It stopped commenting at home, and never spoke at all in her therapy office—although maybe that was because she had no qualities there, but was pale, transparent, a vessel for other people. True, when a client once looked at the cream-colored walls and said, rather angrily: "This place feels like one of those panoramic Easter eggs," she felt offended. But this was only for a moment and then she felt neutral again. She was therefore surprised when the voice spoke one evening after one of her favorite clients, a middle-management executive in his early thirties, looked at her directly and said, "You know, I hate to say it, but something in here feels tilted."

"Tilted?"

"Yes. Tilted. As though, if you stayed here long enough, you would start to think about things in a different way."

Things ARE *tilted, said the voice. That is the way it is in offices these days. Animals don't have offices. But watch them explore your home! Indeed, they may be aware of more than you know.*

After her client left she watched him disappear down the street, wheeling his bike as though it were a fragile part of him. Then she lay on the floor and looked at a small crack in the ceiling. It was quiet, restful, and she liked the feeling of the plush white rug against her hair. In a few moments there was a knock on the door. It was her client again, bike and all.

"I got worried about you," he said. "You shouldn't be in your office with your door open. Last week a woman was killed because of that. I read about it in the paper." She wondered if he'd known she'd been lying on her office floor and supposed that he did, because, in spite of secrecy, everyone knew everything.

"I'm fine," she told him, "really fine. But thank you."

You did the right thing, said the voice. It is nobody's business but yours that you sometimes use your office for private, unusual purposes.

After this episode, the voice didn't speak again for many months. She looked at uneaten eggs, poetry reports, Dungeons & Dragons books, clothes in closets. She argued with her best friend about whether or not laundromats promoted a deeper sense of community and gave a paper called "The Paradox of Psychotherapy," in which she maintained that learning how to be a client involved learning the same peculiar steps needed to function in modern society. "For this reason," she concluded, "psychotherapy may be a questionable and perverse form of socialization. We shouldn't overlook other solutions." Several people walked out.

It was after two Jehovah's Witnesses came that the voice spoke again. *Don't condemn them*, it said after she had turned away two women in clean white suits. *They are just innocent human beings trying to make sense of things. Doomsday is one of many options.* While the voice spoke, her son was at a D & D book, making copious notes about a unicorn. The notes stated that the unicorn had an IQ of 800 and the strength-potential of twenty men.

"How do you figure it out?" she asked.

"You roll some dice," he answered as though she were extremely stupid.

"And then?"

"And then you create a character."

"And what does the character do?"

"It plays with other characters. What else?" Her son looked at her like she was crazy.

"Nothing. I just wondered. Listen: Could you make me a character?"

"Well, not really...."

"Why not?"

"You're a grown-up. Grown-ups aren't characters."

"Why not?"

"They don't change."

Oh, but they do, said the voice. *They just use other options. Try page 79 in that book called* Dungeons & Dragons Part III.

That night, when her son was asleep, she snuck into the dining room and looked at page 79 in *D&D Part III.* She saw a picture of a woman who was half beast and half woman, crouched on all fours like a dog and covered with fur. The caption explained: *Women who grow fur are sometimes feral and live in caves. At other times they stay at home like contented pets. Because of their familiarity with human life—as well as their unpredictability—they are never suitable characters for D&D adventures.*

She shut the book, but not before looking at some runes her son had drawn. One was shaped like a woman, another like a mouse. From the bedroom, her husband called, "Alice! Alice!" For a moment her name sounded strange and foreign.

Her husband was sleeping quietly. He slept on his back the way he always slept, as if ready to greet the world. She got up, went to the bathroom, looked in the mirror, and then bent close to her arms, listening to her skin.

It was an incredible act of will, this growing of fur. She grew it at night, concentrating on one subcutaneous layer at a time and thinking of each pore as a single strand. In a week, two black hairs curled from behind her ears; two weeks later three black hairs curled around her ankles. In a month she had soft, curly strands in patches on her back. She began to wear baggy clothes to sleep.

"Are you planning to sleepwalk downtown?" her husband asked one night when she got into bed wearing tights, a sweatshirt, and socks.

"Maybe," she said. "I might have plans."

"What do you mean maybe?" He pulled her to him and she pulled back so he couldn't feel her ears. "What's going on with you?" he asked.

"Nothing. I just get cold."

"Seriously. What's wrong? At dinner you look into space. And the other day I went to your office to take you out to lunch and you didn't even answer. I know you were in there. I heard you."

"I was with a client. You heard us talking."

"What about the Jehovah's Witness pamphlets, then? Why do you keep them now?"

"Because you never know."

"Know what?"

"What will help. What will give you information."

"What kind of information do you want?" He let her go and leaned back against the pillow.

"I don't know. Maybe I don't want any." She felt fur behind her ears and touched it furtively. She took comfort from its softness. It was like touching someone else.

Thank goodness the fur didn't appear on her face. She continued to see clients and was relieved when the middle-management executive said he was thinking of leaving. "What can therapy do for you, anyway?" he asked. "Give you back to the world," she offered. Her client coughed his nervous little cough, then patted his bike, which he always brought inside because he was afraid it might be stolen. "My bike is my only joy," he said. "I haven't met my one-and-only yet." "You're lucky you have something that brings you joy," she answered. "A lot of people would envy you."

"What are you thinking about, Mom?" asked her daughter one night at dinner.

"Oh, nothing, sweetie. Just stuff. "

"What stuff, Mom?" her daughter asked.

"Just stuff honey. I don't know. Did you finish that report?" There was a piece of rice on the table and she wanted to lick it with her tongue. There was also a chicken bone on the floor. She wanted to scramble down and eat that, too.

"Sure, Mom, ages ago. You read it."

Her husband looked at her evenly. "Are you all right?"

"Yes. I'm fine."

By late winter fur began to grow around her neck and she couldn't risk sleeping with her husband anymore. "I'm sorry, but you're snoring a lot," she said one night. "I think I'll sleep in the extra bedroom."

"Are you sure?"

"Yes, I'm sure. Just for a few nights."

The bedroom was near her son's room, and as she went

to sleep, she heard his toads bleat from their separate rocks in the glass aquarium. They seemed lonely, bewildered, caught in a matrix that didn't suit them. She was glad she wouldn't be a reptile.

It was lonely sleeping by herself. Sometimes she dreamt she was a four-tongued beast with three heads, many claws, and fire-breathing eyes. Once she was a dragon on a dangerous, time-bending mission. When she woke, she sat up in bed, rocking back and forth. Sometimes she remembered her favorite client, the one with the bike. What would happen if he wanted to come back to see her? Would he try to track her down? Think how things were tilted? She leaned close to herself in the dark, listening to her skin. She heard something growing, the way farmers talk about hearing corn.

Growing fur was such a supreme act of will that she didn't notice the day she become an animal. It took the shriek of a neighbor to let her know that something had changed. It took the cry of the mail carrier to send her running to the house on all fours. She sat in the hall, panting on the braided rug, then bounded to the mirror. She saw long black hair, topaz eyes, an enormous black nose, floppy ears. *I have become a dog,* she thought. *But I don't even know what breed I am.*

Dogs are simply dogs, said the voice. *They never bother to think about what breed they are.*

Now her husband pets her gently, not able to explain to anyone, not even to himself, that in some innate sense he knows the four-legged animal is his wife. He's hired a housekeeper who's efficient, humorous, kind, and has never talked to their children about what happened to their mother. In truth, when she was growing fur, she never thought about her children. She never thought she wouldn't be able to help them with their homework, or she'd have to let them give her baths and watch her slurp food from plastic bowls. She'd only thought of a life uncharted by maps, a life more suited to cliffs, and caves. Yet now that she's a dog, all she wants to do is lick them.

No one seems upset. Her children still do homework and go to parties. Her husband continues work as a paleontologist. And since the housekeeper won't answer the door for the Jehovah's Witnesses, they slip their doomsday pamphlets through the mail slot and she can carry them to the kitchen in her mouth. Right now it's a late spring evening and rain is falling outside. She sees their house reflected through the window, hears the howl of another dog on another block. She also smells gradations of dirt and earth beyond anything her family could understand. Her husband scratches her head, her son strokes her ears, her daughter says "good dog"—and all the while they're doing human things—small, meticulous things, essential to continuing human life. Her fur is long, black, luxuriant, and her children put their soft blond hair against it.

"Good dog," says her daughter again. Everybody holds her close.

T HE LETTER WRITER

He had once worked in Hollywood as secretary to Howard Hughes and was able to write the letter that everyone wants to receive—the letter that leaves one with a profound sense of being known. His letters were definitive and often gave people a sense of being seen in the depths of their souls—always in a way that moved them. After getting his letters people did uncharacteristic things like giving up important careers, walking through Beverly Hills naked, and adopting strange animals. Movie stars threw away fan mail. Magnates stopped opening telegrams. One woman hired an immigrant from Baja to tear up all of her lover's letters on Sunset Boulevard.

His letters had the effect of making mail from other people irrelevant. They opened people's eyes to the fact that there had only been one letter they'd ever wanted, and all those days of waiting for the mail had been motivated by this singular, unknown wish. His letters explained the universal appeal of the envelope—an appeal that often turns to disappointment once the envelope is opened.

His letters were always written longhand, in elegant, slanted writing. They contained genuine praise—not effusiveness—and often referred to events that made people feel close to their history. He always ended on a note of poignant lyricism. Nothing was ever contrived.

He himself was ordinary—I can't stress this enough. He traveled incognito, referred to himself only as D.—and I met him formally only once when Howard stopped by his place to pick up a love letter he wanted me to have before I went on a cruise. His suit was dark. His tie was conservative. His sunglasses seemed pressed against his eyes. And he had the kind of monochrome face whose hair and skin seemed made of the same color. He handed Howard the letter without looking at me. I read it on the cruise and realized that D. had seen me so clearly, I'd never be able to lie to myself again.

People speculated that when D. was alone, or possibly with friends, he acted outrageous. In public, however, his manner was epistolary; whenever people saw him, all they ever thought of was the word *letter*.

He was said to work in promotions. That's why Howard hired him in the first place. It was probably in 1933 when he first called D.s' office, and said:

"You'll be writing a letter to close the airline deal."

"I don't do that sort of thing," D. said. "I don't do that sort of thing at all."

"You do now," Howard answered.

D. wrote a letter that resulted in a multi-million-dollar deal. Soon, however, Howard understood that D.'s talents were so beyond the ordinary, he pushed him beyond sales and into love. Howard could get into any woman's pants with D.'s letters—but just once, because after women realized it wasn't Howard who'd written, but a ghostwriter, they began to look for D. If only Howard had understood the range of D.'s powers, he could have made an empire based on the knowledge of human souls. When women began to drop Howard, however, he fired D. in a pique. This was hardly D.'s downfall: By now he was in demand.

D. worked at night, because he said night was when he could discover how people needed to be written to. He explained this to his housekeeper from Jamaica, a woman who kept amulets in the kitchen for luck. It was past midnight, he was writing in his study, and she came to serve him ginger tea.

"Why night?" she asked, as she handed him a spoon.

"Because," he said tersely, "there's a lining in the sky that opens up and tells me stories."

"True ones?"

"Oh yes. Except real information is never the point." He looked at her carefully. "There's something like a cosmic intelligence out there," he said. "I'm not responsible for what I write."

"Of course not. No one is. But does this thing ever write to you?"

"No. "

"Why not? Don't *you* ever want a letter?"

His housekeeper was tall and straight. He imagined her balancing a basket on her head, walking through a market. "Wouldn't you like a letter?" she asked again.

"Not really," he said. "Would you?"

"Oh, no." She tapped her heart "I get my letters from the ackee tree."

His letters always told people things they'd suspected about themselves and thought they didn't want to know. Yet what a relief it was when they discovered that they really did want to know, after all. Just think of the thing you hide from, think of its terrible shape, and you'll have a sense of what this man was up to. There was only one problem: after getting one of his letters, people hungered for more because they were informed, but not satiated. Lives were ruined, spent waiting for his mail. Some people got post-office boxes because they said that after getting one of his letters their own mailboxes assumed a numinous electric charge that frightened dogs and annoyed neighbors. Indeed, when D. was in his prime, waiting for his letters was what one did in Hollywood.

The conversation with his housekeeper haunted him. She was right, he thought: He'd like to get a letter from himself. One night he stayed up late, looking at the sky. Nothing poured from its stars.

"You should go to the ackee tree," his housekeeper said.

"Or take a walk. Do you remember that movie star who came to see you? The lady with the big fur coat? She said she went on walks and thought of what you'd write to her."

"I really don't like walking," he said.."The problem is I'm just not someone else—someone who isn't me. If I were, I could write the letter."

"How could you be someone else?" said his housekeeper, laughing. "How in the world?"

One night, instead of writing to famous people, he began pulling names from the phone book. He didn't mail the letters, but threw them on Sunset Boulevard, and the next day there were mobs of ordinary people sorting through envelopes, looking for their names. At this point he had to be put away. His housekeeper drove him to the asylum and left him with packets of ginger tea. Before she left, she hugged him and said someday he would find the letter he was looking for.

It was Howard who wrote him that letter. He wrote it when D. had been in the asylum for seven months. This letter told D. who he was in a way no one thought Howard was capable of. It was a letter from one recluse to another, telling him about his soul. Howard's fingernails were long by then: the letter was hard to read.

None of D.'s letters are on display, nor is Howard Hughes's letter to D. These letters are private, meant only for the reader. The linguist Jacques Derrida once said there is only one book, known as The Book, and all other books are just attempts to approximate it. Because of D.'s work, it's been proposed that there is only one letter, known as The Letter, and D. alone discovered how to write it. His work was an impossible vector, one that reached its limit.

STAIRWAY TO THE STARS

When they were in central Mexico, they saw a sign by some stairs that said: *Escalier aux Etoiles.* The stairs were wrought-iron black and spiraled upwards to a small apartment. The sign was blue on white enamel.

"What does it mean?" She was slumping over her enormous belly, exhausted from the heat.

"It means 'stairway to the stars,'" he told her. "Don't you know? *Escalier.* Stairs. *Etoiles.* Stars."

She shrugged. She should have known. He was always translating for her.

"How odd," she said, "that the sign is in French, not Spanish. How odd that the stairs have been given a name."

"Let's go up," he said. "See what they're all about. Maybe there are even some stars up there."

"Oh no. It's a private house. We can't go there."

"Why not?"

"Because. It's private."

They always had the same argument. He wanted to camp in a cornfield: she said they might get shot. He helped himself to a dozen Meyer lemons: she said "Oh my God no, they don't belong to us." *The world is my home.* He often said that. He spoke in the comfortable, easy manner of the privileged. He assumed the imperious friendliness of someone who has grown up with maids, chauffeurs, cooks. Whenever anyone served him, he always asked their names and then he would use them. "Sally, I'd like some more salt for this omelet. Marv, I'd like you to check the oil level on the car."

At last they agreed that he would go up, and she would wait below. It was always how they settled these arguments. After he went up, she looked carefully at some flowers in pots along the sides. There were roses in terra cotta, and dark wooden containers with small blue flowers that looked like alyssum. He'd once told her the name of the blue flowers and she had forgotten. She pretended to be interested in the flowers. In a moment she heard a curse, and a man yelling in Spanish, "Get out of here, balls first! You heard me. Follow your dick or I'll cut it off." She heard running and the sound of a shot. Then he was in front of her, sweating, panting, saying, "Oh my God, there's a maniac upstairs, a guy who says he's living in heaven." He grabbed her hand, and they ran down the cobblestone street, she with her enormous belly.

"Come on! Come on!" he kept saying. "The guy's a nut. The guy's a nut. He thinks he's an Aztec God."

Later, in a cafe, where they ordered manzanilla, he told her the man wore a silver mask. One of those sun-god things with rays all around it. "He was standing right there on his patio waiting for me. And then, when I came up, he said his house was heaven."

"Maybe he meant haven," she said.

"No. Heaven. I understand Spanish."

"Well maybe he is an Aztec god. Besides, you disturbed his domicile." She was surprised she had used the word *domicile*. It sounded odd, strangely legal. Her belly felt enormous, as though holding the man's vengeance. Her hair seemed electrified, taking the form of a silver headdress.

"Believe me, that was no God, just some beer-bellied guy with an attitude." He had a tic that came on, unbidden. It happened now: his left eye began to twitch.

Recently she'd begun to slump, forming a cradle for the baby. She took a sip of her manzanilla and sat up straight. "I think he was someone you knew," she said.

"What do you mean?"

"I don't know," she said, not knowing what she meant but knowing she was on to something. "Someone you've met on one of your forays."

"Forays. What the hell do you mean by that?" He stared at her through hooded lids—there was some way he knew how to pull in his eyes. He looked smart and dumb, like an owl. The tic stopped.

"Oh you know: forays into fields. Forays into lemon groves. The kind you take. Domains that don't belong to you." *Domains. Domicile.* She couldn't believe her language. The sun had melted a dangerous place inside her. She wanted to walk through town, letting the women pat her belly, hearing them say *Encinta! Encinta!* as though she were ignited, burning, and they could see it. She wanted to buy a hundred silver chains.

That night, in their pension, he kept staring out the window. He'd already disappeared twice today, ducking around corners, peering into bars. When he looked outside, he seemed to become part of the dusk itself, as though he could float over the red-tiled roofs until he found whatever he wanted. Finally he asked: "What do you mean by forays?"

"I told you. Those times you just barge onto someone's property and take whatever you want. The times you pick those flowers—the blue ones—what are their names?" She was sitting propped on a chair, not understanding her Spanish guide book.

"This is Mexico. I'm here to see things."

"You do it everywhere."

"The world is my home."

"I know. You always say that. I don't agree."

"Whatever." He turned around, no longer blending with the shadows, picked up a copy of *La Prensa*, and suddenly was enclosed in perfect air—air that was sent to him whenever he needed it. The conversation had taken a wrong turn, bringing them to something old, unspeakable. She knew he wanted her to pursue it so he could figure out what she knew. *I'm living behind glass,* she thought. *And the notion of* forays *includes territories I haven't dreamt of.* She decided to ask him nothing.

After he fell asleep, she poked around his pockets, looking for clues. It wasn't the first time she'd picked her way through his pockets in cheap hotel rooms. Sometimes she discovered things, registered them, and then forgot. Tonight all she found were a few pages of *La Prensa* containing uninteresting news: vanilla was being recalled by the Mexican government because it contained impurities that could bring on allergies. A recent survey showed a five per cent decrease in the use of environmental face masks to protect people from the dust in Mexico City. She had no idea why he'd saved these pages. Nor did she have any idea why she could read Spanish so easily. *Defecto. Vehemente.* The words danced in front of her eyes.

While she was reading, she heard three distinct knocks on the door. They weren't hurried knocks. They belonged to someone who knew how to take his time.

"Who is it?" she called.

"The man your husband thinks is an Aztec God," said a voice in perfect English.

She opened the door and saw an ordinary man. He was tall, dark, about her age. He wore jeans and a perfectly pressed white shirt. His only claim to being extraordinary were his eyes: They were blue and piercingly beautiful.

"How do you know he thinks this?" she asked.

"Because. I heard him from my landing."

She let herself into the hall, shutting the door. There were fourteen doors on this particular corridor. Anyone could step outside and see them talking. She realized she was wearing nothing but a large white shirt, reaching to her knees. She bent her knees and the shirt grew longer.

"Why did you come here?" she asked.

"To answer your questions," he answered.

"I don't have any."

"Well, you ought to."

"What about?"

"Your husband's improprieties." The man spoke calmly, without malice. He had the detachment of a scholar.

"How did you know we lived here?"

"I followed you on your walk."

"Why?"

"Because you're beautiful."

She sensed a shift in the atmosphere. The air, previously thick, became thin, without horizons. There were no points of convergence, yet collisions might happen anywhere. She looked at the man: the hairs on his eyebrows seemed alive. "I have to ask you to leave," she said.

"Why?" he seemed puzzled.

"Because," she said in careful Spanish. "I am married. Also, I am pregnant." She pointed to her stomach. "There's a baby in there."

"So you don't want to know?"

"I know enough. You don't travel with someone for as long as I have without knowing everything about them."

"Your choice," he said. "And maybe your mistake. I happen to have something that might help him."

He bowed and made no sign of leaving. She went inside and closed the door. The clarity of air vanished. She saw mounds of clothes, indistinct photographs. The pages of La Prensa were where she'd left them but now she couldn't understand a thing. Maybe her fluency in Spanish never happened. Maybe it was a freak of hormones. She looked more closely and saw several telephone numbers scribbled in the margins of the newspaper. Two were in Mexico City. Three in California. She walked to the door and pressed against it, speaking softly. "I'm coming out to meet you," she said.

The man mumbled something like "Good." She went to the closet and pulled on tights, sandals, found a shawl. As soon as she opened the door the air resumed its powers of convergence. It propelled them past all fourteen doors. It pushed them toward the lemon-scented night. He brought her to his house and they climbed the stairway to the stars. It was long, curved, she could see the whole village through the banisters. Before she entered the lantern-lit hall, she decided she would tell this man that her husband was a drug addict. She decided to tell him he visited apple orchards and lemon groves to shoot up. No doubt the man already knew. She wanted to tell him anyway. She also wanted to tell him that whenever they traveled he looked for messages, codes, signs on houses—anything that might lead to a deal.

He held her arm carefully, as though he knew what she was going to say. He opened a door and led her to a room with adobe walls and opulent furniture. A terrace was close to the room. Outside, stars were everywhere, pressed against the sky like flowers. She sat in a leather chair and looked at them. They were large, close, preternaturally bright.

He walked to a kitchen and poured her a glass of water from a bottle. "You aren't used to the water here, are you?"

"No, I'm not." She sipped for a while, considered what she wanted to say, and realized she'd changed her mind. "Really, I should get back," she told him.

"To him?" he asked. "And to what he does?"

"It can't be worse than what you do," she said, looking at the pictures, the statues, the leather chairs. "There's no way you'd know, unless you were a part of it."

The man didn't disagree. He rose, and held out his arm. No information passed between them. He hadn't even kissed her. They walked back on cobblestone streets, warm from the afternoon. At the door of the pension he pressed a package in her hand. The package was wrapped carefully in rough white cloth. The pressure of the man's hand conveyed a confidence, a secret. "You'll give this to your husband, won't you?"

"You came all the way for *this*?"

"Of course. I know when someone is in trouble."

She didn't ask who was in trouble and he didn't say. He bowed and walked slowly down the street. Tomorrow she and her husband would go on other walks. Tomorrow they would visit other houses. She walked upstairs and he was waiting for her by the window.

"Where have you been?" he asked.

"Getting you what you need," she answered.

R UNNING IN PLACE

They had the fight about the washing machine on a cold
day in mid-December, three weeks after their baby was born. A
surprising sienna flower had bloomed between them, yet they
were fighting. She said she couldn't stand laundromats, and
besides, they needed clean clothes for the baby. "All those cute
little jump suits," she said. "All those things they gave me for
the shower."

He waited until she opened her eyes. "I love laundromats," he said. "They help me keep my sanity."

"I don't get you," she said, shaking her dreadlocks. "Man,
you are lost."

He'd been born on an Oregon commune in the sixties.
His parents raised sheep and carded their own wool. She'd
been born in a Los Angeles ghetto and was the first in her family to go to college. They'd met at an art opening, where she was
showing inner-city murals and he was reviewing the show. "I
bought the wine for this," she'd told him, "and I made damned
sure it was decent. When my kids come to see their murals,
they drink in style."

Now he looked at her evenly. "Washing machines at home
keep people from gathering," he said. She laughed like he'd
made a joke.

"Those damned laundromats. I hate them. They remind
me of the ghet-to." She said *ghetto* so he could hear the *t* in the

middle. He said she was affecting an English accent. She said he didn't understand irony.

"Let me tell you something," he said. "Laundromats are the only thing in my life that ever made me feel normal. It was the only time I went to town. I put my hair in my shirt so no one would see how long it was and I read old *Superman* comics and got candy from the vending machine. And those machines where you put in dollar bills and get more money, not less. I even told the attendant I was Presbyterian. Laundromats saved my life."

"Well, let me tell *you* something. All they remind me of is taking my little sisters to get their clothes washed while my mama was working. Watching them ask for candy. Having some guy pinch my butt. Relaxing? I don't think so."

The baby began to cry. "I'll make you a deal," she said, picking her up. "I'll buy the washing machine and you take your clothes to that laundromat." She underscored the word *buy* in a street-wise way. He imagined her holding up the attendant from Nicaragua at his favorite laundromat and carrying a big white machine to their car.

"I wish you'd stop talking about the ghetto," he said. "Maybe you were born black, but I had other problems."

"That's what they all say. But let me tell you, being born black is not an option."

She bought a washing machine and dryer the next day. When they were installed in the basement, she took the baby in her arms and did a dance, stopping to touch the dials.

"There's Fluff and Perm-dry and Normal," she said. "And it makes me happy that there's even Mini-Wash. No saving for a big load. And now I'm going to wash that jump suit my sister gave us."

"Just don't wash my things, okay?"

"Hey, I wouldn't touch them."

Soon she came to the living room and stuck a bundle of clothes in his face. "Aren't they nice? They're something else."

He stuck his face in the bundle. The baby's jump suit was covered with nubs of fabric. Her white socks were rough. "They smell like a spray they used at the commune that made everything smell like processed wool," he said. "They smell like little stuffed animals."

"You know what it is with you? You don't risk anything, that's what. You lived with those weird people and now your head is messed up about putting yourself on the line." She sat on the floor and folded clothes. "Your head's messed up," she said again.

He told her to shut up, and she said she wasn't going to say anything else anyway.

She folded the clothes like origami: she crossed the arms on the baby's jump suit, like they were holding something and curled up her socks like spoons. She carried the clothes inside and talked to the baby: "I got your little jump suit all clean. It's soft and pretty like a cloud."

After dinner, he went to the garage and began to run in place. It gave him an exhilarating feeling of thrust, like he might go out the ceiling. The washer and dryer ran with him—huge boxes of soap and white American dreams. He hit his feet on the wooden floor. The washer and dryer rattled and shook.

"For Godssake, what are you doing?" she said, sticking her head in the door. She was holding more to wash—a pile of maroon towels.

"Running in place. It's good for me."

"Running in place? My God, I've been doing that all my life."

"Are you sure? You have a kid, a washing machine, and you sign your name to almost every mural in the city. And you buy whatever the hell you want."

"Shut up," she said, more softly than she'd ever spoken to the baby. "Whatever you don't know won't hurt you."

She was crying and he acted like he didn't see. He took her in his arms and they started to dance. Her dreadlocks

101

shook, his shoelaces came untied. The basement floor danced with them. "Looking good," she said to him. "Looking *good*."

Afterwards he went upstairs and gathered his dirty clothes.

"What are you doing?"

"I'm going to the laundromat."

"I thought you'd like the washer and dryer. I mean, they belong to all three of us."

"I do like them. It's just this thing with me. Steam. Soap. Dollars that turn into quarters. Those carts that float. And the attendant from Nicaragua. All those things. I like them."

He went to the dresser where he kept his dollar bills and counted out five very carefully. Before he left he gave the baby a kiss. "Someday you'll see for yourself," he said.

FROZEN CATS

It was an old ritual by now, burying frozen cats under the pear tree in their backyard. Their first cat, a yellow tabby named Asuncia, died while they were in Mexico, and their cat feeder, a student in mechanical engineering, had frozen her remains. When they came home and unwrapped Asuncia, she was gold, beautiful, perfect; her icy fur gleamed with eternal life. They buried Asuncia under the pear tree and then his wife got the idea that all dead animals could be frozen. "It's better," she said. "Better to wait till you're ready to say good-bye." Her parents were Irish and used to hold wakes. "It has nothing to do with that," she said when he reminded her. "It's something else. Something I can't explain." She pressed her hands in anguish that struck him as theatrical. "Humor me," she said. He did.

After Asuncia, they froze all their other cats who died, waiting a month, two months, even three, before putting them in the ground. In addition to Asuncia, there was Freddie, Clara and Ramon—a black cat who gave him the creeps because there was a distinct erotic current between Ramon and his wife. Thank god they were vegetarians. Otherwise the cats would get mixed up with the frozen meats. The summer his sister stayed with them, Ramon was in the freezer. His sister camped in their basement, played old Carole King tapes, and criticized their lives according to doctrines of est. "Would you mind burying Ramon?" she asked one day. "I'd really like to freeze a chicken. Besides, you guys have so many *incompletes* in your life. You really should prioritize." "You don't get rid of something the minute it dies," his wife said peevishly. "Why not?" asked his sister. "Because," she answered. "Timing is everything."

The day his sister left, they buried Ramon under the pear tree. As soon as the earth was covered, his wife ran to the house and began to hit pillows on their futon. "I'm tired of cats," she said. "I want to have a kid." He nodded, stroked her hair, didn't know what to say. He didn't want children. She did. An old, tired argument.

Now they did have a kid—Stefan, who was three—and another was on the way. Yet here they were still, freezing dead cats. This time it was Gloria, a glamorous tabby who died at the age of eighty-one, not before peeing on the dining room table and sending twelve guests to a cold porch on New Year's Eve. While he dug Gloria's grave, he imagined strings on his hands making him perform unnatural acts. He wondered if Gloria knew she were frozen.

"She's beautiful," said his wife, looking at Gloria. "I mean she looks so *real.*"

"She *is* real," he answered.

"What I meant is, she doesn't look dead. It must be the fur. When you look at the fur it's like they're still alive." His wife leaned against the pear tree and began to cry. He knew he should comfort her and kept on digging.

Stefan, who had not been born when the other cats died, looked at Gloria curiously. He had his own little shovel in case he wanted to dig, and he used the shovel to touch her. "Why is Gloria so hard?" he asked.

"All things get hard when they die," said his wife, "but Gloria is extra hard because she's frozen."

"For God's sake," he said to his wife, "leave it alone."

"No," she said. "I want Stefan to know the truth: We kept Gloria in the freezer until it was time to say goodbye."

"How come" said Stefan. "To help her get better?"

"No," he said. "It was definitely not to help her get better."

"Will you shut up?" said his wife. She folded her hands

and looked at Stefan. "What I mean is," she said, "we wanted Gloria to look exactly the way she looked when she was alive."

Stefan looked confused. "But her eyes are weird."

"Ice keeps things pretty much the way they were," he explained, glaring at his wife. "You know, like frozen peas." Stefan looked blank.

He turned to his wife and whispered: "I resent having to tell him this stuff. It's not the kind of thing a kid should know."

"Screw you," she whispered back, "you're always telling me how to live."

Stefan ignored them and petted Gloria with his hands. "Her fur is so soft. I want to save it."

"That's a great idea, honey," said his wife. "I'll get scissors, and we'll cut some off." She went to the house and Stefan leaned close to Gloria.

"Gloria," he said, as though she could hear him. "Gloria, we're going to bury you."

He could tell from the sky it was going to rain and had the crazy idea that if he didn't dig fast enough, water would fill the grave. He dug quickly, afraid he'd find bones of Freddie, Ramon, Clara, and Asuncia. He was relieved when he kept hitting dirt.

"Do you like burying Gloria?" asked Stefan.

"No," he said. "I don't."

"Why not?"

"Because I loved her. Even when she started to pee on tables."

Stefan laughed and began to dig a hole with his own shovel. She came back with scissors, cut a piece of Gloria's fur and handed it to Stefan, who wandered off. When Stefan was gone, he pressed her against the pear tree. "We've buried so many frozen cats under this damned tree," he hissed. "Isn't it time we just buried them as soon as they died?"

"How can you be so heartless?" she said. "I mean it's like your stepmother telling me she was going to cremate your

105

father. There he was, sick with pneumonia in that hospital room, and she'd already made arrangements with the Neptune Society."

"Will you stop talking about that? It happened years ago."

"No!" she said in a whisper. "I mean I'll never forget that day when you were out of town, that awful day when your step-mother called and said your dad was going to die and she'd already arranged to have him cremated, even though he wasn't even *dead* yet. And there was Ramon in the freezer, just inches away from the phone. The *contrast* between her dispassion and our caring. The complete and absolute *contrast*. How could you forget?"

"I can't. Not with you around."

Stefan came back. He was holding Gloria's fur against his cheek. "Is she unfrozen yet?" he asked.

"No, honey. It's time to bury her."

The hole was deep. They wrapped Gloria in a flannel blanket, lowered her to the ground, sprinkled roses on the blanket and covered it with earth.

"Say good-bye," said his wife, who was starting to weep.

"Bye-bye," said Stefan, waving.

When the grave was covered, Stefan went back to his own hole, began to dig with urgency and hit something hard, covered with grime. Maybe it was a bone—some silent admonition from all the cats who'd been frozen for far long. But no—it was a Lego soldier, and Stefan began to brush it off.

"I found something!" he cried. "Something I've been looking for!"

CAPTAIN CRUNCH

Every morning Captain Crunch gets up from his room at the other end of the house, strides into the breakfast room and says hello to his wife, even though she's still asleep. Captain Crunch has been having an affair with a woman in a far-away state—a woman with generous breasts and a pocketbook like Queen Elizabeth. He's always used their house as a *pied-a-terre*, and before this woman there was another woman and no doubt there will be a different woman after this one. Nonetheless, the Captain is cheerful. Another day. Another cereal.

While Captain Crunch has coffee, his wife stays in bed as late as she can. Her dresser is filled with rings from cardboard cereal boxes and her mirror still has autographed pictures of Captain Crunch. He likes her to wear the rings, all twenty-seven at once, but only at parties: *I want you meet my wife*, he always says at parties. *She's a well-known translator from German, Russian, French and codes from various cereal-boxes.*

At the last party they went to, no one bothered to pretend it was a party. The injunction to "network" was right on the invitation. While Captain Crunch spilled cereal on the rug, she tried to get translation gigs. Cereal from Captain Crunch is still considered lucky, so she had to make her pitch while people were groveling on the floor.

In addition to his hat and boots, Captain Crunch was wearing a cape. It flew over the smoked salmon, and made the breadsticks sway like wheat. It forced an actress with reconstructed breasts to fall on his starstudded boots. Captain Crunch's wife looked at an almost-boyfriend across the room and their eyes said, *let's pretend we did and not*. Afterwards, on a street that reminded her of Schenectady, Captain Crunch explained that he still enjoyed going to parties with her even though he really loved his girlfriend. He came home and ate a huge bowl of cereal.

While he ate, she finished translating a French essay called *The Multi-Dimensional Aspects of Love*. In it, the author proposed that the spaces inside of people are the same as spaces inside other four-dimensional objects: when you twist a person, he proposed, some hollow place inside them buckles and is never the same again. He then described a snake he'd seen on a Paris street—a beautiful, liquid garter snake that had been twisted and mauled by a cat. *Snakes are fluid*, he wrote. *They are liquid, and seemingly simple. This liquid skin conceals a life-force much closer to our own. We must never forget this fundamental truth.*

She showed the essay to Captain Crunch who said he'd never understood the Gallic mind. Then he told her he'd gotten a letter from his girlfriend, a letter that was touching. *You have no idea how good it feels to get laid*, said Captain Crunch. He put his head in his bowl of cereal and began to cry.

TRAVELING CLOTHES

I decided to see my second husband when I went to visit New York after living in California for fifteen years. He had been a drug dealer and became so rich he retired at forty-one. It pissed me off. He had retired while I was busting my butt to make a life. For different reasons, each of these facts upset me. What if Aaron looked old? Or what if he'd turned square and played golf? What if I, who had stuck with making pottery, looked hapless? There were other things I didn't think about either—like the fact that Aaron and I had gotten married and later I had forgotten about it. "Forgotten? How could you have forgotten?" This from my current husband, the third one. "I don't know, I'd just forgotten, and then suddenly I remembered. Marriage is like that. These days, I mean. Irrelevant, interchangeable. Except for you."

When I called Aaron to tell him that I was coming to New York, I didn't mention our marriage on the phone.

"I'll be so happy to see you," Aaron said. He didn't sound retired at all. He sounded charming. I raced to a local bookstore and bought him all three volumes of *The Genesis of Fire*. Nothing was too good for him. I hid the books from my husband.

When Aaron met me in the lobby of my Greenwich Village hotel, he didn't look old at all. He was wearing a dashing fedora, just like he'd worn when he was a drug dealer and he still reminded me of Dashiell Hammett. We smiled, crackling blue electricity arcing between us, and as we walked towards Soho, the night rose about us—festive, reckless, redolent with air of countries we'd always meant to visit, countries where dust was red as blood and the buildings faded rose. *Were we ever married?* I wanted to ask. *Tell me, Aaron. Were we?* But I didn't. I held his arm, and we walked through the unruly night until we found a bar that served extravagant tapas. I ordered a glass of red wine and Aaron ordered Italian sparkling water. Aaron was in AA.

"Are you happy?" he asked, raising his glass.

"Yes," I said. I showed him pictures of my son, who was eight, studied karate and had been photographed wearing a headband. In one photo my son had piercing eyes that made me feel that he was looking through me. Suddenly I felt uncomfortable.

"I've worked hard," I said, "to make a life for myself."

"I'm proud of you," said Aaron. "And I'm sorry we never went to India."

It was only time he ever acknowledged that we had a past. I gave him *Genesis of Fire*. Aaron seemed sad that he hadn't brought me anything.

I'd forgotten what happened to the air when we were together. It could blow us to heaven like a flying carpet. It could blow us right into a bedroom. It could do that right now. But Aaron didn't ask me to his apartment. It was no longer the walk-up we'd shared in the West Village, but a loft that had belonged to a famous painter. A friend had given it to him. "It's in a constant state of disrepair," Aaron said, when he dropped me off at the hotel. "Otherwise I'd love to have you to dinner."

I wondered if it had a false floor, concealing bundles of marijuana, the way our old apartment did. "Are you really retired?" I asked.

"Yes. I made a bundle. So I quit."

I was going to an artists' colony in Vermont, and would later return to visit gallery owners in New York. I'd brought clothes for my trips to these galleries—a crimson skirt, a dark jacket, a black velvet dress—clothes my son called "lady clothes." They felt alien and cumbersome,

"Would you mind keeping some of these for me?" I asked Aaron, not even knowing if he had a closet.

"Oh, sure!" he said, "It would be my pleasure."

I handed him a suitcase, and had a lonely, tugging vision of his apartment. *It was so nice to see you,* I wrote from Vermont, *and so nice of you to keep my clothes.* As I wrote, I remembered Aaron leaving me at the Port Authority bus terminal. Quick kisses. Promises to visit. Dust that could blow him to Vermont.

As soon as I got back to the city I called, and Aaron brought me the suitcase right away. Thank God, I thought, not knowing why. Later, when I opened the suitcase there was only one white blouse in it, a blouse that didn't belong to me. My velvet dress was missing.

"I didn't see a jacket or a dress," Aaron said, when I called. "In fact, I have a distinct vision of only one hanger."

"A hanger? There wasn't any hanger. I gave you everything in that black suitcase."

"But I saw a hanger," Aaron said. "Is it possible that one of them slipped off?"

"Just how many hangers did you see?"

"I don't know. Maybe one."

"Well I couldn't put a dress *and* a jacket on the same hanger. Aaron, listen. I have to have that dress."

There were several such calls. We talked about dishonest cab drivers, our precipitous rush to the Port Authority, what a nuisance it was to hang up clothes, and why I might have hung them up after all, even if I didn't remember. The air continued to blow around me. Our metaphysical speculations grew more baroque. I remembered similar discussions we'd had years ago: the merits of covering the false floor with pine board or oak; whether black bean soup was better than white; whether tiny stitches for hemming marijuana bundles were preferable to big ones. It was the cocaine that had done him in, I thought as we talked. It was the cocaine and his trip to India. All at once, I said to him: "Hey, Aaron, were we ever married?"

Aaron laughed nervously. "You *know* the answer to that one."

"Well, whatever," I said, "just go look in your closet."

"Believe me, I've looked. I've turned everything upside-down."

"Please, just do it again. They're my only grown-up clothes. I have to go to galleries."

Aaron put down the phone, went to his closet and I could hear the clattering of metal. *Is he into chains?* At last he came back and told me he'd found nothing.

"Can I come over and look?"

"I'm embarrassed to tell you my house is a mess."

That night I slept badly. At seven in the morning Aaron called.

"The jacket fell out of the closet," he said. "Literally. I opened the door and it just fell out."

"My God! Was there a belt?"

"Yes!"

"And the dress and the skirt?"

"Not yet."

"I'll come over and get them right away."

"No. I'll come to you."

Aaron arrived at eleven, an hour before I had to go to the first gallery. The jacket was crumpled but passable, I raced out and bought a pair of black leggings. The gallery owner was a short, owlish man in a dark blue suit. *I'm all wrong,* I thought. *I wish I had my funky velvet dress.* I rolled up the sleeves of the alien white blouse to try to look more casual. I wanted my dress more than I wanted an exhibit. I could see the dress on the floor of Aaron's closet, or maybe buried under another false floor, reeking of marijuana. After I left the first gallery, I walked through the city and found a dress almost like it in a shop that was owned by a man from India. This dress was longer, more elegant. The muted pattern was the same.

"Do you have it in a shorter version?" I asked. "I gave it to a friend and he lost it. The one he lost was short."

"Not shorter," he said. "But if you buy longer and he finds shorter, you do not repeat. Anyway, I'll take off fifteen dollars."

I bought the dress and wore it out of the store. A dress of redemption. A dress of velvet dust.

"How in the world could he have lost your dress?" asked my husband when I came home. "And by the way. Do you suppose Aaron's wearing it?"

My husband was holding one of my scarves. He twirled it, looked at me, and then I remembered—me wearing one of Aaron's fedoras, Aaron in my purple dress with spaghetti straps and a pattern of embroidered umbrellas. We'd gone to a party where Aaron did an Isadora Duncan dance using one of the hostesses' scarves, which eventually fell in a punch bowl.

"Well?"

"Okay, okay. It could have happened. Sometimes we did exchange clothes."

Like several things between Aaron and me, the exchange wasn't quite even. His clothes were big on me, so when I took them off it was like I'd never worn them. But when Aaron wore my clothes they looked like wrinkled skin.

"What happened?" said Marvin Linski, when I brought the purple dress in to his shop to be re-sized.

"A friend of mine wore it."

"A friend? You call this a friend?" Marvin was a thin, intelligent man, with blue numbers tattooed on his arm. In order to survive he'd developed X-ray vision: no doubt he could guess who'd been wearing the dress.

113

"Promise me you'll never let this friend wear your clothes again," he said.

"I loved that dress," said my husband. "I'm sorry you don't have it anymore."

"What about the long one?"

"That other dress was short. When you wore it with red tights it was a knock-out."

After he said this, my husband sat on the living room couch drinking wine. Because he wasn't an alcoholic, like Aaron, he was able to drink half a bottle without blinking. It was a very old red wine, and left sediment at the bottom of the glass. He swirled his fingers in the sediment and said, "Now some creepy drug dealer is wearing your velvet dress."

I almost told my husband what had happened the last day I saw Aaron. We were at an espresso shop eating pastries and Aaron confessed he hennaed his hair.

"I look younger than anyone I know," he said. "So why not keep it that way?"

After that he'd stuck his tongue out at me. His tongue had an extraordinary number of cracks in it and in that moment, Aaron began to look like a piece of parchment instead of Dashiell Hammett. I was sure he had the dress. I was also sure we were married and bound in a love-knot forever.

"What are you thinking?" my husband asked.

"I don't know," I said. "About the air that blew me to this living room, I guess."

In the Middle of the Night

He called and asked her to come over because he thought he was going to throw up and he might be dying. It was well past midnight and the call didn't wake her because ever since he'd left, over a year ago, she couldn't sleep. She wasn't surprised that he called. In the past, when they still lived together, he'd often said, "If I were dying I would come to you, because there's something about you that would make dying bearable." He said this sincerely, and she understood: there was something about her that contained the grief of other people.

"Please explain more," she said to him. Her tooth was slightly infected, and she could feel a swelling in her mouth like a gum drop. She worked her tongue around it while they talked.

"I told you," he said, "I think I'm going to throw up."

"Are you sure?"

"Yes. I can't believe it."

For Yoav, throwing up was the same as dying, and much worse than being put into an iron-maiden, or impaled by hundreds of swords, although those things had never happened to him. He was so afraid of throwing up, he'd gone through great feats to avoid it, even in Costa Rica where both of them had eaten a bad lobster dinner.

"How do you not do it?" she'd asked from her bed in their tiny, depressing room.

"I use the power of my will," he said.

He had last thrown up was when he was eight. He'd been at his cousin's in Long Island and eaten far too many éclairs.

Now, after twenty-five years of evasion, the game was up.

"Get over here quickly," he said. "Please."

She didn't say yes right away. They'd broken up almost a year ago and the leave-taking wasn't pleasant: an abortion she hadn't wanted. A sweet, gawky new girlfriend named Sylvie who played the cello without a shirt. And a terrible scene on the street in which she ran into him and Sylvie by accident, and managed to drop half the contents of her purse in front of them. Sylvie had gentle eyes, wore a short black skater's coat, and her cello case hung from her arms like a friendly dog. Yoav's picture had still been in her purse. She'd bent down to pick everything up and Sylvie had looked at her with pity.

"Please," he said again.

"All right, I'll come."

While she got dressed, she looked through the apartment to see what she could bring. Yoav had never moved his things out in any official way, and occasionally came back to find whatever occurred to him. Just last month he'd spilled a drawer full of papers on the floor, and the month before that she found seven odd keys scattered on the dressers. She decided not to bring him anything she cherished. She decided she didn't want to bring him anything spiteful either because she took her mission to squire him through throwing up rather seriously. Finally she decided on something neutral: Yoav was a vibraphonist and used a lot of mallets. Their padded ends were soft, like stuffed animals, and, in his haste to leave, he'd forgotten most of them. She was always tripping over them and a guy who had a crush on her once asked if the mallets were sex toys. "No!" she'd said, and chased him out of the house.

For tonight, she chose three light-blue mallets, even though a set made four. Then she put on a long Cambridge scarf from another boyfriend, a man that Yoav hadn't liked. "He's *mishugeh*," Yoav always said, whenever she wore the scarf.

She took a cab to his new apartment and Yoav met her at the door. His face was pale, making his black hair darker.

"Well, I did it," he said. "I just did it in the sink."

"Congratulations. "

"Spare me. It was a dreadful, dreadful event. Much worse than I ever thought it was going to be." Yoav was wearing a dark kimono, and the bottom of his black mustache was wet in a way that made her recoil.

"Maybe you should drink some water," she said. "It helps get rid of the taste."

"I did drink water. It didn't help."

Yoav looked forlorn, and his black eyes, which were often fierce, seemed terrified. She knew he wanted her to say something comforting. Something like: *For most people it isn't pleasant but for you this is the equivalent of Auschwitz.* She didn't.

"Maybe you should drink some more water, anyway. Really, it often helps."

"I can't stand your impersonal kindness," Yoav said. "It's like you're taking care of Arnold Anybody." Yoav had complained about this before—her distant, measured compassion.

"Well I've never been to Arnold Anybody's house. Not since he walked out on me."

"Please," Yoav said. "Be kind."

She saw he was trembling. The back of his silk kimono was embroidered with an enormous yin-yang sign that was heaving back and forth like two fish.

"All right. Truce," she said, and walked into an apartment she'd never seen before. Everything was clean. The whole place smelled of lemon wax. She took off her scarf and put it on a birch chair where Yoav could see it. He noticed and seemed uncomfortable. This made her happy.

"Why would drinking water help?" he asked, like a child wanting to be told a fairy tale. She didn't want to talk. She was far too busy looking around. Absently, she said: "Well, first of all it gets rid of the bad taste. Second of all you're probably dehydrated."

She hated herself for spelling it out. Yoav nodded obediently and went to get water. Again she saw the yin-yang pattern on his kimono. His back looked bearish, elegant, awkward.

"Would you like some water, too?"

"No, not really." She was deathly afraid of throwing up herself and didn't like the idea of drinking from a glass that Yoav had touched.

"Are you sure?" he said, looking at her with reproachful eyes. "It's great water. It's from this special spring."

"Okay. Just a little bit."

He served her water from a blue container in an octagonal-shaped glass that was interesting to hold. She walked around the apartment, pretending to drink it.

Except for his vibraphone, everything was different. There were black chrome bookcases, low birch tables with smooth, weathered surfaces, and a bean-bag chair covered with cloth the color of a musk-melon. "It's clean," she said, dropping into an enormous beige couch, which puffed and billowed around her, like a person, scooping her up. For a moment she lay back, feeling comforted.

"Do you like it?"

"What?"

"The couch."

"Everything but the color. It's a little drab. Listen, do you have a maid?"

"Well, a cleaning person. She comes every week."

"Hattie?"

"No. Someone else."

At their old apartment Hattie Dunsley, who called herself a maid, not a cleaning person, had been sent by Yoav's mother from Long Island. She hadn't liked the idea of a maid and after Hattie left on Fridays she usually messed the place up.

"Hattie's not doing a good job," Yoav sometimes said.

118

"She's tired," she would answer. Later, usually in the mornings while Yoav was still asleep, she scrubbed, swept and puffed pillows. It was part of her secret, furtive domesticity.

"I think I'm going to again," said Yoav.

"What?"

"Throw up."

"Well it's the best thing to do, it you have to. Really. It ends up making you feel better."

"Will you come with me? Hold my head?"

"In a minute. I mean there's a lot to absorb here." Her words released something and he disappeared. Sounds were heard. Sounds she didn't like. There were postcards on the desk and some checks that belonged to a woman named Eve Sommers, a name she'd never heard. The checks were bronze-colored and "Eve Sommers" was written in cursive script. The checks had Yoav's address on them.

"Who's your maid?" she asked, when he came back, looking shaken. "That friend Hattie was always talking about? That woman with the seven kids?"

"How can you ask me something like that now?"

"I don't know. I guess I can't be compassionate on command. Anyway, who is it? Sylvie?"

"No, not Sylvie. Sylvie's out of the picture." He cleared his throat and looked around. "Noah sent someone over." Noah was his music manager. He was always sending someone over.

She wondered who Eve Sommers was. Again she remembered meeting Sylvie on the street, her warm eyes and dog-like cello.

"What about Eve? Does she help clean, too?"

"No. Eve runs a health-food store. You always said I'd find a macrobiotic cutie."

She never remembered saying anything like that. She wondered where Eve was now. Had she fled when Yoav thought he was going to throw up? Was she not good with the infirm or dying?

"I didn't know Eve moved in," she said.

"She hasn't. Those checks are a cover-up. She needs an address."

"Poor Eve."

"Spare me." He sat on the beige couch. She looked at it closely and noticed it was covered with special carelessness, falling in sculpted folds.

"Is that supposed to be unveiled?" she asked.

"No. It's shabby-chic. The latest."

"And what else is the latest?"

"These forks." Yoav got up from the couch, went to the kitchen, and brought over forks with black, wrought-iron handles. She didn't like them, but wished she owned them anyway.

He sat opposite her. It was one fifteen in the morning. His new bronze clocked ticked away. "It's been a long time," he said.

"Yes, it has." She reached into her pockets and brought out two of the mallets. "Here. I found these."

"Oh God. I'm sorry. I should come back and pack." He took the mallets and used them to tap a chair.

"I thought you did come: I thought you came back last month and emptied a whole bureau drawer."

"I was looking for my passport."

"Well next time let me know. I mean how could you do that? How could break in like this was some sort of storage bin for your past?"

"Look, I let you have the apartment. The least you can do is let me get my stuff." He'd left with his passport and a dozen silver spoons that belonged to his maternal grandmother.

"So," she said. "Your gigs. How are they?"

Yoav didn't answer, but stared into space. The space he stared into wasn't ordinary space. It never had been. It was filled with singers with tufted pink hair, rings in their noses, opaque eyes. Concert halls in Prague where kids in leather jackets reached to touch him. Also musical notes. Yoav said he could see them at a distance, just like a visual artist can see perspective. As he stared, he belched.

"Oh God, it's going to happen again! Please come hold my head this time. "

"Yoav, don't ask."

"Why not?"

"I can't explain."

"Please."

Soon she was in his bathroom, holding Yoav's head. She held it the way she might have held a child's head, one hand on his forehead, the other cradling his hair. She looked in the other direction, so she wouldn't get sick. Everything in the bathroom was dark teal, except for touches of maroon. She saw three maroon toothbrushes in a holder near the sink. One of them was small. When they left the bathroom, she asked: "Who has the small toothbrush?"

"Edmund. He's Eve's kid. He's three."

"I thought they didn't live here."

"They visit. Edmund's cute."

"Wow. There's your forks, the beanbag chair, and Edmund's toothbrush. What else is new?"

Yoav didn't flinch. A flush came over his face, a look of pleasure and excitement. "Actually, something's very new. I did my book over."

He was talking about a book he had written for the vibraphone. It had been lost, buried in the old apartment. "Where is it?" he often asked. "I have no idea," she answered. Once his father had called. "Yoav wrote a valuable book," he said. "It's not exactly the answer to the stock market, but it has good stuff in it. Maybe you could look for it." "I've looked," she told him, not mentioning the socks, pencils, mallets, that cascaded at every turn. "Just look one more time," said his father. "It means everything to him."

"Would you like to see the book?" Yoav asked.

"Yes," she said. She was trembling.

She got into bed and he handed her a manuscript full of musical notes. It was called *Exercises for the Vibraphone*. Yoav's notations were unusually neat, not like anything else about him. "The scales," he had written, "are an ecosystem of sorts, and exercises must take this into account...." She saw the date: January, 1992, one year after he'd left her.

"So. You wrote it over."

"Yes." He looked at her evenly, and she looked at the forks, thinking she found them attractive. They belonged to an age of craftsmanship, when people took their time and cared. She began to like the couch as well. It looked the way a couch would look if it had a secret life as an animal. She sat on it carefully and found that it held her up. The absence of shape was all in the covering.

The clocked kept ticking. It was almost three in the morning. She saw he didn't want her to go.

"It's been a long time," he said .

"Yes, it has," she said, just like she'd said before. She reached into her pocket and brought the other mallet out. "Surprise!"

"I get it," he said, taking them. "I should come back and pack."

"We've been through this. Maybe I should go."

"No. Stay. I still might have to throw up."

"What about Eve?"

"She won't be here. She's with Edmund."

"Ah, yes, Edmund. You have a kid now."

"Let's not get into that."

They'd always slept together. In the middle of the most brutal fights, in the throes of the abortion, in Germany with two single beds in rooms the size of spindles—wherever they were, they always found a way. Now it was easy. The shabby-chic couch folded out, its creases made soft curving corners. They slept side-by-side, the *Exercise Book for the Vibraphone* on the table next to them. Yoav's long careful hands touched hers softly, just the way he composed on the piano. She touched her tooth, which she had never mentioned. She could feel the swelling had subsided. At four-thirty there was a phone call from Eve. Long pauses. The sound of sobs. She got up, relieved she was still dressed.

"Listen, I've had it. I better go."

Yoav didn't answer, but stared into space, perhaps at more musical notes. "Just tell me one thing. Did you burn my first book? The one I left."

"No. Your stuff is in such a shambles I could never find it."

"And what about those clothes?"

"No. Not them either."

"Well, thanks for coming."

"No problem at all. I'm glad to be the patron saint of barfing."

"Spare me."

"Try thanking me again."

In the cab going home, she wondered why Yoav had called. It was her empathy, she supposed, an empathy that went beyond spite, an empathy that transcended other moments, like that time she'd taken a razor to his lambskin coat when he went to play a gig the night after her abortion and later she claimed she couldn't find it. The early dawn air was thin, drawn out, breathable by just a few stately prostitutes. Traffic lights clicked on and off with the precision of a Mondrian painting, and the cab driver drove a green-light dance, not stopping once until he reached her apartment.

"A perfect ride," he said to her as she got out. "You get those once in a lifetime."

SILVER

I'm always impaling myself on silver things, things my lover gives me when I'm not looking. He buys me silver rings and puts them on me when I'm asleep. He buckles my waist with a silver belt, drapes me with silver necklaces, fastens anklets under my jeans, puts six earrings in the holes of my ears. Silver and never gold, because silver is the color of the accident one longs for. It's light that slants through rice paper shades, a face on the street that carries you through the solstice.

You can't love someone without hurting them—that's what my brother told me once. We were home from college, washing pots in the sink, and my brother had just gone crazy on LSD. He thought he could climb walls, when he was only scaling a chair. He thought he could see the truth, when he was staring at a shopping list. "But one thing I knew," he said. "You can't love someone without hurting them. I saw that when I looked inside my brain and all the cells were singing, *You can't love someone without hurting them*. They were beautiful, those cells. All of them were made of silver."

My parents were getting divorced, just as I am now. Light was coming through the kitchen, the kind of light that makes you think you're in another century. "Is it fifth-century Greece?" I asked my brother. "No," he answered. "It's the Han dynasty."

I wanted to hug my brother and say everything would be okay. His brain would stop singing. He wouldn't have to hurt people he loved. In fact, things didn't go well for him until he got a Ph.D. in physiology and discovered that all those years of watching his own brain cells had paid off. Now he lives in Rome and writes papers with titles like *The Neurophysiology of Indifferent, Compatible Systems.*

Sometimes I wake up at night, impaled by silver, and think about my brother, far away in Rome. I think how he's found love, and hurt a lot of people in the process. I also think of my lover in a small beige room, surrounded by flowering trees. I lie in bed alone, wearing heavy silver.

"Why don't you take those off when you go to sleep?" my lover asks, touching the scratch marks on my arms and neck. "For God's sake, what are you doing to yourself?"

I don't answer, because then I'd have to tell him about the random silver of his face the day he stepped out to meet me. *Your face was like that,* I would have to say to him. *Don't you remember? It was the day before the solstice, people were racing around to buy presents and you stepped forward to meet me. A week later you gave me a silver bracelet. A week after that you gave me silver keys. But none of this would have mattered if your face hadn't been an accident.*

THE ENCHANTED BOYFRIEND

They couldn't help worrying when they opened the living room door. He was lying on the couch and looked still as a statue.

"Who's sleeping?" they asked, holding tight to their coloring books and crayons. "Who is in there sleeping?"

"Never mind," said Mauve, who was Dee Dee's sister. "You don't have to know who he is to know that you shouldn't go in there." She went upstairs, flouncing like she was a pair of curtains, and they had no other choice but to look more closely. They saw a young blond man, about eighteen, maybe two years older than Mauve. He wore a white T-shirt with a tear on the left sleeve and blue jeans with a bulge in the crotch. His hair fell across his face, and his body was still except for his left hand which trailed along the side of the sofa, the way a hand trails in the water. They went closer and closer until they smelled sweat on his shirt, and a sweet, warm smell of soap.

"He looks like he's sleeping," said Christine.

"He doesn't look real," said Dee Dee.

When Mauve fluffed up her hair it meant that she was going to use a curling iron and make faces in front of the mirror for a long time. But this time she came back in a hurry, looking more like a movie star than usual because she was wearing a low-cut purple sweater with tight jeans.

"I told you not to go in there," she hissed. "I told you it was none of your business." "

"What's his name?" asked Dee Dee.

"Never mind," said Mauve.

"How come?" said Christine.

"Oh for god's sake," Mauve said. "His name is Jer." She said the name *Jer* very low as though whispering the name of a god.

"Who's Jer?" asked Dee Dee.

"Don't say his name," Mauve hissed. "It's not your business to be on familiar terms." She left the living room and this time didn't ask them to leave. They heard her running water in the kitchen and sat solemnly on the floor. Mauve was probably cooking dinner.

Jer shifted on the sofa, so his arm made an arc along the green rug. He sat up and looked around, except he didn't seem to be looking at anything at all.

"Don't watch him," Dee Dee said to Christine. "He could bewitch us."

"Nonsense," Mauve said. "He can't bewitch anybody." She sat next to him, and held a warm towel to his forehead. "You see?" she said. "He's not bewitched. He's moving."

"He doesn't like it, though," said Dee Dee. "He's frowning."

"Will you bug off?" said Mauve. "I told you not even to look at him for God's sake and now you're gelling me he's bewitched." Her eyes got dreamy and precise, the way they did when she was thinking about a new sweater. "He plays volleyball on the varsity team," she intoned. "He's great at trigonometry." She said this as though it were in a special part of her head, the part that made lists of all the places she wanted to visit. While she spoke Jer fluttered his eyes.

"Not true," he mumbled. "None of it."

"Sure it's true," Mauve said. "Jer's modest. Hey, Jer, honey? You want some soup?" She put some cold canned soup close to his nose. "You had a little fall, hon. You're going to be okay."

Jer opened his eyes and looked at Dee Dee. "Hey there, blue eyes," he said.

"Shh!" said Mauve to Dee Dee. "One word and you're out of here."

She held the spoon to Jer's lips. "You want some, hon?"

"Uh-uh. I'm not hungry." Jer looked around the room. "Do you live here?"

"You *know* I live here," said Mauve. "You picked me up for that movie. "

"Oh yeah," said Jer. "On the porch. Right?"

"Right," said Mauve. Her face got large and gave off light like a moon. "Dee Dee," she said, "you better go now. And Christine, too. Jer's not feeling well." She fluffed up a pillow like she was a nurse.

"Don't make them go," said Jer. "They're your sisters, right? They're cute." He looked at Dee Dee. "Do you like Barbie and Ken?"

"I like Skipper."

"For crying out loud," said Mauve. "Will you two just go away? And anyway, only Dee Dee's my sister. Christine's just her friend."

"So?" said Jer. "They're still kids. Why can't they stay?" There was an edge to his voice.

"Because they bug me," said Mauve. "And besides, they have crazy ideas about you. They have crazy ideas about everything. They happen to think you're enchanted."

"Well maybe I am," said Jer, sitting up on the couch and looking more focused. "All kinds of things happen to people they don't know about." He looked at Dee Dee. "All that paranormal stuff. You know that word?"

"She doesn't," said Mauve, "and even if she did, she couldn't explain it."

"Let her try," said Jer. He held Mauve's arm, his forefinger moved back and forth against her skin. "Let her try," he said again.

"It means you feel stuff other people can't see," said Dee Dee, who had just seen a movie about a teenage psychic who was a nerd until kids found out she could predict the scores of all the football games. "Sometimes you know what's going to happen. Sometimes you know everything that did happen. It's *beyond*," she said. "It's about beyond." She liked the way *beyond* sounded. She heard it echo in the room and imagined it like a cave. "Beyond," she said again. "And the third eye."

"You see?" said Jer. "She's not so dumb after all." He winked slowly. A wink as long as a heartbeat. "And what's enchanted?" he asked Christine.

"That's easy," she said. "That's when someone looks you in the eye, and you fall asleep for a hundred years or just forget who you are and where you're supposed to be going. It used to happen all the time. Sometimes it happens now. And cobwebs always grow around you."

"You understand" said Jer. "Really, I'm surprised." He looked at Mauve—a long, reptilian gaze—and pulled some fluff from his T-shirt. "That was a cobweb," he said. "Right from my own castle. You think I'm kidding. You think I'm putting you on."

"I don't know what you're doing," said Mauve. "I only know I want you to leave."

"You want me to leave?" said Jer. "You bring me home with this injury and lay me on your couch and now you want me to leave? Well screw you." He got up, wobbled, and sat down again. "Well I can't leave," he said. "I'm enchanted. You have an enchanted man on your hands. What are you going to do about it?"

"I think you're drunk," said Mauve. "I think you were faking that sprained ankle and you're drunk."

Jer lay back on the couch and pulled the quilt over him. "Think what you like. Your sisters are smarter than you."

"Like I told you only one of them is my sister," said Mauve. "The one with the big mouth."

"Well, whoever they are, they know. They know all about it." Jer looked at Dee Dee and she felt like the plush white bear she cuddled in the dark was inside of her. Jer's voice was soft, reminding her of men and women asleep at banquets, the kind she'd seen in fairy tales.

"I know," she said, wanting to kiss him, violently, fervently and gently, so he'd always sleep on their living room.

Christine shifted, and Mauve said, "I can't stand one

more minute of this." The door opened and Opal Brannon walked in. She was a big-boned woman who wore outrageous hats that made Mauve never want to be seen with her on the street. She was home late from her job as secretary to Amos Goodall, the only honest lawyer in town, who kept his records clean and never tried to pinch her butt, even though he plied her with eggnog at every Christmas party.

"What in the hell is going on?" she said. "The four of you look like zombies." She took off her hat and walked over to the couch. "Aren't you Jerry?" she asked. "The one that Mauve wouldn't let in the house when she went to that party at the Moffet's?"

"His name is Jer, Mom," said Mauve. "And there wasn't time for him to come in. We were late."

"Well, why is he sitting here?" said Opal Brannon. "And why is the water boiling away on the stove?"

"Because he sprained his ankle," said Mauve. "He sprained it at volleyball practice." Dee Dee and Christine were still. They wanted to explain how Jer was enchanted, but were sure Mauve would think of something dreadful to tell Opal about them, like the time they'd peed underneath the porch just to see whether it made a sound hitting the earth. To their relief, Jer said it for them.

"Mrs. Brannon," he said, "my ankle feels fine. I just have no idea how I got here, that's all. And besides I can't seem to leave. It's almost like I'm enchanted."

"My God," said Opal Brannon, sitting close to him on the couch, as though his T-shirt weren't torn and you couldn't see the bulge in his jeans. "Do you know where you live? Do you know your name? I mean maybe you have amnesia. People get that all the time." She looked at him through her brown mascara. Jer looked back without blinking.

"I know everything," he said. "I even remember this house. How Mauve wouldn't let me in when we went to that party, even though there was plenty of time. I remember everything. I just can't get my bearings." Opal Brannon leaned close. Her perfume filled the room like a meadow.

130

"Do you want me to call your folks?" she said. "Maybe they could come get you."

"Oh God," said Jer. "They wouldn't believe me. They'd think I was nuts." He looked upset, maybe for the first time.

"Do *you* think I'm nuts?" he asked, and, before Opal Brannon got a chance to answer, he pointed at Dee Dee and Christine. "*They* don't. But they're just kids. What do you think?"

"I don't know," said Opal Brannon. "As far as I'm concerned, enchantment is a subjective state. Amos was just working on a case where someone thought he was put under a spell and made to sign a will." She looked Jer in the eye. "Were you hypnotized?" she asked. "Was there some creepy teacher at school trying to get you to do something? Some coach who wanted you to shoot a thousand baskets?"

"Mom," said Mauve, "he plays volleyball. *Varsity* volleyball."

"Well there's nothing for it, then" said Opal. "I'm going to have to kiss you." And she did. She got on top of him, and put her arms around him, and kissed him for a long time, the way Dee Dee thought she would have. Jer's long arms with golden blond hairs circled Opal Brannon's waist, and Mauve went to a beat-up purple chair and curled up into a ball.

"Maybe they're going to do it," Dee Dee whispered to Christine.

"Maybe," Christine whispered back.

They didn't. Opal Brannon pulled away, and smoothed back Jer's blond hair. "Too many people love you," she said. "None of them know who you are."

He nodded and fell asleep. Opal Brannon got up quietly, and took her packages into the kitchen. "Some dinner you make," she said. "Thank God I picked up soup. Amos told me to. He said, 'Opal, you're going to drive yourself crazy, if you depend on some teenager for supper. Do what I do. Get a microwave.' Well, I wouldn't do that. That's just too much. But the new deli with all those tiny vegetables has great soup. So I got some."

131

She set the kitchen table, just four places.

"Won't Jer eat with us?" asked Dee Dee.

"He certainly won't," said Opal. "He'll sleep for a while, and then he'll get up, and walk out the door. And you"—she pointed at Mauve—"if you're smart, you won't talk about it to him at all, unless maybe someday if the two of you get together, and he mentions it you won't deny it, but only in passing. But believe me: only in passing. Now get some soup bowls. This is great minestrone."

"Mom!" said Mauve. "I can't believe you. It's like you think I'm naive or something."

"She is," said Dee Dee. "She didn't know he was enchanted."

"You be quiet, too," said Opal. "Why shouldn't I know? I might be the only one to understand."

"Why?" said Dee Dee.

"None of your business," said Opal. She laid out soup in a white tureen that Amos gave her when his wife left and the town was buzzing that he'd ask her to marry him. It had a pattern of lilies. A noodle fell in one of the cracks.

"Now look at that," said Opal, pulling out the noodle. "Ruining the effect. Maybe you kids will get me something better for Christmas. Something from Tuscany with those earthen colors. Something from a place I'd like to go someday."

SWEETHEART

She saw him that summer when she was standing in the yard of their rented house near dusk, a time when the bruise of the day and evening sky came together, and the air had the preternatural mist of fairy tales. He was a slight, slim man in his early twenties with large kind eyes and soft black hair. She didn't know his name, or even who he was, any more than she knew that this summer her parents would, in a moment of crazed fury, sodomize her. She only knew she was standing in the dusk, as though it were a real, live thing, waiting for her aunt to arrive from New York City for the weekend. She was wearing a light blue dress, because blue was her favorite color and already—even though her fifth birthday was five weeks away—she'd asked for a birthday cake with blue icing.

Last week she and her parents been sharing another summer house on Lake Placid with a leftist union organizer named Ed, who gutted fish in an icehouse containing three tabby cats stuffed by a taxidermist. His wife, Eva, had bad breath and hated her mother. "You piss me off," Eva screamed, her cigarette breath blasting every word. "You piss me off too," her mother answered.

It was because of Eva that they left, her mother racing to our bedroom and packing their bags as though they were refugees. Yet now they were in Provincetown, as though they'd always lived there—and the quality of light defined a safer world. In this light, the man passed softly. He looked at her cautiously, so she knew she was allowed to look back, unlike the way she felt with most grownups. "Hello, sweetheart," he said to her. And then he was gone. She stood by the gate and looked after him while he walked down the street. *Hello sweetheart.* No one had ever called me that. Just like she'd never had a gate, or a garden—in New Jersey they lived in an apartment. Yet now she had a gate and a garden, both, and was starting to take them for granted. She stood by the gate until the man disappeared.

Moments later her aunt arrived from New York City, laden with suitcases, pumpernickel bread, pastrami.

"Lucia, I am in love," she told her. "A man called me sweetheart, and I have to look for him."

"Can you imagine?" said her mother, as they put the food away. "This man comes by and calls her sweetheart and now she wants to find him."

"Why not?" said her aunt. "You don't meet people like that every day."

"Don't you want a drink?" said her mother.

"No," said her aunt. "If I have a drink, it will get dark, and then we won't be able to find the man." Her mother snorted and lit a cigarette. Her aunt lit one too.

"She said he was lovely," said her aunt between puffs. "She said he was like someone in a fairy tale."

"Everyone is like that at first," said her mother. "Then, of course, you get to know them." Her mother laughed a short, bitter laugh, and she wondered if she meant people like Ed and Eva, or just people you happened to see on the street. Her aunt and mother finished their cigarettes in silence. Then her aunt got up and took her hand and her mother didn't say anything. She was large, sad, dramatic, given to outbursts. Her aunt was thin, wiry, tough, given to withdrawal. During arguments a point came where her aunt grew silent, just like someone playing tug-of-war suddenly letting go the rope: her mother would be lost, rolling backwards on the sidewalk.

She and her aunt walked all over Provincetown, by the quays, the waterfront, the shops. They walked as she imagined children in storybooks would walk, with a sense of purpose, holding hands. The dusk loomed before them, fading into the

134

ocean. Twice she thought she saw the man: it was always someone else. "No one but you would do this for me," she said.

They never found him. The man had vanished like a
prince called away on some urgent mission.

"Maybe he was just a visitor," her aunt said.

"No," she said. "He lives here."

She was right. Two days before they left Provincetown, the
man passed the gate again. Once more he looked at her quietly
and said: "Hello, sweetheart." Then he was gone. This time she
knew not to follow. A week before her birthday, she'd experi-
enced an act so perilous, so angry, so loud, it split her apart,
leaving a cavern of vast, dreadful space inside of her. Since then
she'd become a curious sort of listener, ignoring words, inter-
preting meaning from sound. And the sea was now filled with
a strange, poisonous salt. A few days earlier she'd watched a
friend's large, amoebic body fall in rhythm with the waves and
known that she herself wouldn't feel safe enough to swim for a
long time. The blue birthday cake, nearly impossible to order,
had been obtained at great expense, and she wasn't at all surprised when it arrived because she always got the little things
she wanted.

ROSSETTI'S CLOSET

Six years after Lizzie Siddal died, Rossetti began to pay secret visits to her closet. This was long after he, Swinburne and Meredith decided they didn't like living together. And long after he'd broken ties with most of Lizzie's friends. Except for his housekeeper—a woman named Mrs. Beehawken who had known Lizzie in happier days and didn't like him much—Rossetti was living alone. He wasn't working, either. He'd put his last manuscript of poems in Lizzie's grave.

When he first moved to the house in Chelsea, Rossetti filled it with whatever he found that he thought Lizzie wouldn't like. She'd liked clean surfaces, distance, a sense of space. Rossetti liked bric-a-brac. In Chelsea, he bought old mirrors, crockery, antique spoons, a collection of cutglass jars. But when it came to Lizzie's closet he made things just the way she had them in their cottage. He hung her chains and lockets from hooks and put her favorite pen on top of an oak chest that Lizzie had bleached white, using an acid. He put her brooches in the chest, and filled jewelry boxes with old keys, pebbles, glass smoothed by the sea. Last he hung up a portrait he'd done of her.

The closet was in his study. "Don't let anyone come in here," he told Mrs. Beehawken. "Not even the maid. I have the wits to clean it myself."

He'd never meant to make Lizzie a closet in his house in Chelsea. He moved there to forget her. But one day he went to the attic looking for a tie-clip he hadn't seen after Lizzie's funeral, and one poem he hadn't sent to her grave with the others. He had the idea they were in pockets of her dresses, which he'd dumped on the attic floor. But when he held the dresses upside-down and shook them, nothing fell out but pieces of cream-colored paper with cryptic notes in Lizzie's handwriting. *Rain again. Must delay the roses.* Suddenly he found himself on the floor, burying his face in the dresses, smelling Lizzie's scent, a mixture of violet and soap.

The closet in his study had a small paned window which gave off enough north light to paint by. Rossetti spent a lot of time there, arranging Lizzie's clothes, supposedly in preparation for doing her portrait. First he hung her black dresses in a single row. Then he alternated them with crimsons, creams and whites. For a while he had a sense of entering a secret world, governed by an unknown order. And then he grew tired of the closet. He bought a collection of empty baskets and put them in the downstairs hall. Next he bought a wombat.

A wombat! What would Rossetti think of next? He did think of other things next. First a jacare, which almost gave him a concussion and had to be given away, and then a mandrill, who didn't like English weather and died. He settled for a tropical fish called an isabelita. She needed special food and warm water and had to be protected from the wombat. Then he began to paint portraits of Jane Burden, the wife of William Morris, and spend evenings alone, looking at Jane's face. It was calmer than Lizzie's, although not as interesting. Once he visited the closet and compared it with an old portrait he'd hung there. Lizzie also looked calm. He left the closet quickly.

Mrs. Beehawken, the housekeeper, called the wombat "that Australian badger." Otherwise she didn't mention it, until one summer evening when the cook served them both burnt pudding.

"I couldn't help it," said the cook, "but that animal started

137

making noises. I knew it could smell the pudding and was trying to get out of its cage and I just wasn't going to deal with it."
Mrs. Beehawken smoothed the front of her dress and picked at the pudding's blackened crust. She didn't say a word. But when Rossetti went to the scullery to get apples for the wombat, she followed him and said:

"Why do you need these animals? Why do you want to live with these awful beasts?"

The scullery was cramped. He could see Mrs. Beehawken's eyes. They looked like currants in the burnt pudding.

"Excuse me, madam," he said. "But I live as I please. You knew that when you came."

Mrs. Beehawken bowed and left the room, leaving opinions in her trail—opinions about Lizzie's increased intake of laudanum, her poems, her art, her vision, not to mention him and the clutter of their tiny cottage. Mrs. Beehawken hadn't been their housekeeper when Lizzie was alive; she'd been a friend of Lizzie's aunt and paid only a few visits. "Stay with me," Rossetti pleaded when Lizzie died. And Mrs. Beehawken did. Even though she didn't like him, and he didn't like her.

After their talk in the scullery, Rossetti went to Lizzie's closet, but not before a sitting with Jane Morris.

"You're thinking about something," she said. "I can tell. Something about the past."

"Not at all. I'm just thinking about your portrait." They were in a small room off the parlor and Jane was in a light blue dress. Mrs. Beehawken was in a nearby room knitting. They could hear the clack of needles.

"No," said Jane. "You're not." She smiled and her eyes grew full of contained excitement. She hurried back to her husband in a hansom.

The closet was just as he had left it. Quiet, and imbued with that secret sense of order. He'd never visited in the

138

evening. By candlelight, the jewelry looked animated. And the dresses seemed obedient and patient, in the simple, quiet way all clothes await their owner. Unlike Jane, Lizzie never thought about style. She looked good in black—a color not thought right for women of her age—but she wore it anyway and it lined the walls like an eclipse. She also liked subtle, uncomfortable transformations—like wetting her clothes to create the impression of draped statuary; or taking sturdy English oak, and dousing it with that acid until it was almost white. Rossetti preferred natural order. But by candlelight, everything looked sturdy, opaque, even ordinary, and this relieved him.

That night he sat on the closet floor, sipping brandy, thinking about Lizzie; how at night they'd pored over books together, her red hair tumbling against the page; how on sunny afternoons they'd walked down lanes, holding paints and brushes, looking for promising scenery. He remembered less pleasant things, too—but all through a haze of brandy.

The next day when he was getting apples for the wombat, Mrs. Beehawken cornered him in the scullery. "Excuse me," she said. "But your eyes are looking rheumy. Are you all right?"

"I'm always all right. And you?"

The minute she turned her back, Rossetti raced to a bedroom mirror and looked at his eyes. She was right. They did look rheumy. As well as dreamy and far-away. *Like Lizzie's*, he thought, *or maybe the way I painted her. That viper thinks I'm taking laudanum.*

But Lizzie's eyes in the portrait were not dreamy at all. They were solemn, astute, as if thinking about what she would need if she returned. The velvet dress. The garnet brooch. And the seed pearls he'd thought of giving to Jane. That night he imagined how Lizzie might walk into the closet, notice the brooch and think, *I've forgotten about that. Maybe I'll wear it tomorrow. Please come back,* he said to the portrait. *It'll be different now. I'll bring the wombat to the zoo.* The face looked skeptical. The eyes withdrew. And now he remembered their arguments in their bedroom where his manuscripts were stuffed in jars, or their parlor where envelopes exploded with bills and books sprouted brushes. "Everything here is a container for everything else!" Lizzie once cried.

One rainy afternoon, a year before she died, Lizzie took the parlor into her own hands. She put papers on bookshelves, crammed books into drawers, stuffed everything else into wooden chests. He came home, dripping wet, hoping for a fire, and found her in a purple chair, drifting away on laudanum. Then he saw the spotless parlor.

"What *deceptive* order!" he said. "I'll never find my sealing wax!"

Lizzie opened her eyes and got up slowly as if guided by an inner map. She floated across the room and felt along the edge of a bookcase until her hands cradled the mound of wax.

"Why can't you live in peace?" he asked, angry that she'd found it.

"Why can you live in peace in a pigsty?" she said, handing him the wax. When she left the room, he threw the wax on the floor. From another part of the house she called, "I've never seen you in a state of calm, Sir. Not once...."

Her eyes grew sharp again. Something in the closet annoyed them. *Clutter,* he thought. *It was that nonsense about clutter that did us in.* And now he started to look for his tie-pin in earnest, shaking down dresses, opening boxes and drawers. He found a piece of cream-colored paper in a chest, but it was blank.

There were noises at the end of the hall—Mrs. Beehawken shifting in bed, as though she were sleeping on a ferris-wheel. He paused in his search, listened. And now he heard another sound—the wombat escaping its cage. It was a small, stealthy

140

sound, like the rasp of a comb against hair.

"It's that animal," Mrs. Beehawken cried out, "It's going to come upstairs and befoul the carpets!"

"I'll take care of it," he said, leaving the closet and going downstairs with a candle. He crawled on his hands and knees until he found the wombat underneath a sink in the scullery. "Come back," he said. "Be reasonable." But the wombat wouldn't budge until he filled its cage with walnuts. The next day Mrs. Beehawken said: "From now on his cage must have a double-lock. Otherwise I won't go near the scullery."

"Then don't," he told her.

The fire in Lizzie's closet was the wombat's fault. One night, after it escaped, and Mrs. Beehawken was saying something must be done, Rossetti raced downstairs. He'd been working on a portrait of Jane Morris, yet felt heady with the notion that Lizzie would return. He ran downstairs in the dark, leaving a burning candle at the edge of her white lace dress. The fire was small, but he made a lot of noise and commotion as he stomped and coughed, using a greatcoat to smother the flames. Mrs. Beehawken ran in, holding a candelabra, and threw water on everything. Rossetti got drenched. So did Lizzie's clothes.

Mrs. Beehawken didn't ask him what the closet was. She knew it was a shrine, and Rossetti was grateful. He leaned against the closet door, and watched her take out all of Lizzie's dresses. He helped her sweep the ashes and put the dresses in the scullery to dry. "It's too dark to put them in the garden," Mrs. Beehawken said. But the next morning she put them outside.

"Best to give them a good airing," she said. "Best to get them a good airing and give them away."

Then she gave him a look, the look of one who does not believe in shrines, and soon he went upstairs and watched the dresses from an upstairs window. The wind blew them so hard, some of the sleeves billowed as though Lizzie's arms were inside them. And that night, when he went upstairs, the closet didn't belong to Lizzie anymore. Mrs. Beehawken had hung up the dresses again and they smelled of thyme, lavender, verbena, and some other, elusive bargain made with the wind. *My tie-pin*, he thought. *I'm sure I'll find it now.*

Two days later Rossetti called Mrs. Beehawken into his study and explained he would no longer be needing her services. He spoke gently and this startled them both.

"It's for the best," she said, "even though the dresses weren't under my charge."

"Would you like some anyway? As a keepsake?"

"I'm much too portly to wear them."

"Then something to remember her by? Some jewelry?"

"Maybe those seed pearls," she said.

The seed pearls were in the closet hanging from a pewter hook, and covered with light grey ash. He cleaned them in the scullery, using a brush the way he'd seen Lizzie clean them. When the pearls turned white they looked fragile. What if Mrs. Beehawken stepped on them with her enormous feet? He put them under her door reluctantly and the next day could see the pearls like small glinting eyes beneath her double chin.

Two nights after the fire, Rossetti dreamt that Lizzie came to his study holding her dresses. They were blowing in the wind, clamoring for attention. She dumped them on the floor and began to complain about the wombat. And then about Jane Morris and her socialist hypocrite husband. Finally she said: *I know what you're going to do. So do it!*

The house was acrid from the smell of smoke. Rossetti woke in a sweat. rushed to his study and recorded a different dream. *It was only a closet*, Lizzie told him. *Really, it was only a closet, and I don't need it anymore.* Then she apologized for all the ways she'd made his life difficult—her grief about their stillborn baby, her complaints about the mess in the parlor. She even apologized for appearing in Millais's portrait as the drowning

Ophelia, because it was more famous than anything Rossetti had ever done. *All those things*, she said. *I understand how you might have hated me.*

It was cold as he wrote. A strong charred odor came from the closet, adding to his sense of chill. He threw a coat over his nightshirt, lit two extra candles and went back to his desk. I have lived to regret my actions, he wrote. *I want to reclaim my poems and continue my life.* He went to the scullery, found crackers and whiskey and stood by the window, eating, sipping, and listening to the wombat, which, at this moment, he loved more than anyone else. He loved it without recourse, without the sense that it could ever give him anything back. He wanted to hold it, rock it, but knew that it would bite him.

Lizzie was buried on Hampstead Heath where there were rumors of intact bodies and wild, vampirous ghosts. Rossetti's requests to exhume her grave flowed smoothly. Papers were signed. Grave diggers were hired. People were naturally curious.

When the poems were exhumed, there was a moment in which Rossetti thought he would never see anything but rich black dirt because the gravedigger was drunk and had trouble locating the grave. However, the poems, entangled in Lizzie's red hair, were intact and so was her body—even bystanders agreed about that. She was resplendent in her black mourning dress. Every jet button glistened. "Peaceful," someone remarked. "Yes," Rossetti agreed.

After the grave was covered, he stayed for several minutes, running his fingers through the grass. "I'm looking for my tiepin," he said to the gravedigger. "Best to let bygones be bygones," the gravedigger answered.

The closet became a half-ruined hole. Some of Lizzie clothes were thrown away, others were heaped on the floor. He gave some keepsakes to Jane, and a few more to Mrs. Beehawken, who had ruined the closet forever. Two years later, in 1871, Rossetti, William, and Jane began to live together in a house in Kelmscott Manor. Rossetti did portraits of Jane and made love to her with William's blessing. He wrote a ballad called Rose Mary, that couldn't be traced to anyone he knew. The wombat died. So did the isabelita. And the poems, kept so long in Lizzie's grave, were published to much acclaim. He titled them, quite simply, *Poems*, and only later wrote a book of sonnets called *The House of Life*.

COPERNICUS CHAIR

She saw him in the evening, during her late-night shift at the Tap Room. It was just after Malcolm called and said he'd be working late.

"Again?" she'd asked, lowering her mouth towards the phone.

"Well yes," he answered, "I think I'm onto something."

"Something small?"

"Something important."

Malcolm was a physicist. He worked with invisible particles. He liked to work at night, when he could be alone.

Ellen paused, projecting silence into the phone. It was a thing she could do, this shaping of silence into something audible. It bothered Malcolm, who said, "Listen, El, don't be mad. And if I find something good, I'll name it after you."

"Don't," she said, ducking to avoid a guest on his way to the bathroom.

"Why not?"

"They don't name particles after people. Besides, I'm already hard to see. And, I was discovered long ago."

"For God's sake, El, you're so dramatic," said Malcolm. And he hung up.

It was then that he came into the bar—a dark slender man in a black T-shirt and jeans, with a folding chair scrunched up like an insect under his arm. *Neurasthenic*, was what she thought. *That man looks neurasthenic.* The chair looked neurasthenic, too, but in a more graceful way. It was a slender, folding

145

beach chair with wood the color of driftwood. The man carried it to the bar and asked: "Is it okay if I unfold this? I want to have a drink."

"Sure," she said. "There's plenty of room." Which was true. Almost no one sat at the bar.

"That's good," he said, setting the chair next to him, "because the two of us have had a very difficult day."

"Excuse me?" she asked, trying to read his eyes. They were sensitive, selfish—or both. She wasn't sure which.

"A difficult day," he repeated, not explaining further as he unfolded the chair—a procedure that was delicate, solicitous, like seeing someone being helped from a cloak, or an origami bird being made to fly. The chair was too long to be wedged between the bar stools. He draped it between two of them, and it looked awkward, like a woman with folded knees. When he was done arranging the chair, he sat on a bar stool, and said, in a voice that was used to giving orders:

"I'll have a glass of dry white wine, the dryest you have."

"We have excellent Fumé Blanc."

"But is it *dry?*"

"Yes. Very dry. Is that good enough?"

"What's gotten into you, Ellen?" said a retired musician with frizzy hair, the only other person sitting at the bar.

"Nothing, Mo. You want another drink?"

"You bet," said Mo. "And then I'll want another. You know me. "

She poured the newcomer his wine, got Mo his whiskey, and drifted to the tables where people were drinking Perrier and eating salads of dandelion leaves and nasturtiums—things that she and Malcolm agreed belonged in gardens. Most of the customers were in their sixties. *Retirees* was the word they used. They were artists, writers, professors, bankers, and a woman weaver of macrame who ordered onions in balsamic vinegar. They came to Vermont for the green, the quiet, and were disappointed to discover that the bells from the old stone church were a recording from a different church, far away in England.

"Ellen," said a retired professor from Manhattan who

liked to pinch her butt, "when are you going to do something with that brain of yours? When will you start to teach instead of talking to us geezers?"

"Whenever," she said. "You know I have a thing about time."

"Time," said the professor grandly. "Do I know about time. Real time. Unreal time. The elusive time of modal logic. But what can you really do with time, except to live it?"

For God's sake, she thought, nodding in a way that was guaranteed to end the conversation. When she returned to the bar, the man with the chair asked: "Was he annoying you?"

"No. We like to talk."

"And what about the others?"

"They're okay, too."

In a sense, she meant it. They all knew she was a dropout from an excellent university and her unfinished philosophy thesis on the logic of imaginary entities was reputed to be brilliant. They also knew she was married to a physicist who liked to work at night and sleep half the day. "He acts like he's on a graveyard shift," the musician once joked. "He should take better care of you."

Ellen moved through the tables collecting empty wine glasses. They were fluted, long-stemmed, doubling for wine and water. The man with the folding chair watched as she dried them and put them on a rack above the bar. Each glass made an extra glint in the mirror. She stepped back to look at the effect, and the man touched her arm: "You're dying to know about my chair, aren't you?"

"No, actually I'm not." She dried another wine glass and put it on the rack.

"You're sure?"

"As sure as I can be of anything." She put away the towel. "Have you come to watch the birds?" she asked.

"No. I've come for the sake of the chair. The city is too much for it. It's too sensitive."

"Please. This is beginning to sound like one of those shaggy dog stories about bars."

"I agree completely," said the man. He leaned close and touched her arm again. "Can you listen with your heart?" he asked.

"Not always. But sometimes."

"Well okay ," he said, his voice dropping lower. "Then I'll tell you: This chair was the first student of Copernicus. And it never got over it. I mean never. This chair"—he put his arm softly on the canvas cover—"absorbed the complete shock of the mind of the 16th century. As well as the shock of Copernicus himself."

"How do you know?"

"Oh... a long story." He sighed and sipped his wine. "A long, long story."

Ellen took a closer look at the chair. It was an ordinary beach chair, striking for its wood, which was white, almost bone-colored. The cover was faded mauve sailcloth, reminding her of sea, surf, inclement weather. If this chair had lived in the 16th century, she thought, it would have been a tall beautiful woman, awkward in heavy gowns, forever stooping under doorways, probably intelligent.

"You know who Copernicus was, don't you?" said the man. "That guy who told everyone the sun was the center of the solar system and upset everybody's idea of things? Well this chair was his first student." He looked at Ellen, waiting for signs of astonishment. She was careful to register nothing.

"Do you know about Copernicus?" he asked. "Do they teach you stuff like that anymore?

"I know a lot more about Copernicus than most people. Anyway, even an informed second-grader could tell you about him."

"I'm sorry," said the man with sudden deference and solemnity. "But I've had a very hard day with the chair. The noise in Boston is too much for it. I've brought it here to rest."

Boston, she thought, getting a vague, inchoate picture of his life. She imagined a town house, filled with books, art,

148

burnished leather desks, the life that she and Malcolm might have someday, if he discovered something small enough. She looked at the man and he was looking at her with an almost frightened intensity.

"Would you be willing to serve the chair a drink?" he asked.

"Of course," she said. "Does it like the same dry white you do?"

"The chair doesn't know what it likes. It only understands the gesture."

She poured more Fumé Blanc and set it before the chair. She half-expected the chair to shift its bone-like wood and take the glass. Nothing happened. The wine just sat there.

"It doesn't know how to drink," said the man, taking the glass himself. "But it can sense and appreciate your kindness." He drank the second glass quickly, then said. "This chair was in a state of permanent shock because it had been the first to hear from Copernicus that the earth was not the center of the universe. The very first," he said, shaking his head.

"The first student is always the one who bears the shock of the master," he continued. "The master makes the discovery but needs someone, or something, to absorb it. By the time the second and third and fourth students come along, the master feels at ease and they take the information well. But the first student must always carry the terrible raw shock of the first moment. Do you understand?"

"Yes. I understand." Almost against her will, she remembered that Copernicus had known about the solar system for years before he told the world. Indeed, the treatise that severed the 16th century from its own bones had been published while he lay dying.

"What are you thinking about?" said the man.

"Nothing. I mean what is there to think? You tell me this chair has a history and I have to accept it."

At the other end of the bar, she saw Mo lean forward, straining to hear. His wild, unruly hair that concealed permanently frazzled thoughts. She had the disturbing sense that he

149

was about to say what she'd almost said before, could almost see the words forming at the end of his hair: *In the days of Copernicus there were no such things as folding chairs. The furniture was monstrous. You needed three servants just to get a footstool from one room to another.* She walked over to the Mo and leaned against the bar.

"Do you want another whiskey?"

"No, not yet. I'm fine." He gestured toward the man. "A kook, *nu?*"

"No. Just a guy with a chair."

She brought Mo another Jim Beam anyway, and he grew quiet. Yet until he loped out of the bar, she could feel the words bursting inside him: *In the days of Copernicus there was no such thing as a goddamn folding chair. Well, of course there wasn't. The damn thing came from Macy's.*

"What's bugging you?" said the man with the chair, after Mo left.

"Nothing," Ellen answered, "Why?"

"Because you look like you're walking on eggs."

"Walking on eggs is a habit with me." Ellen noticed Mo hadn't left a tip.

"What other habits do you have?"

"Being married, for one. And talking about chairs, for another."

The man seemed nonplussed. "You also talk about time," he said. "Time is a thing with you."

"How do you know?"

"Oh. I heard you when you were clearing a table and waving that pompous ass off. That was clearly an ongoing conversation you have with him. Wasn't it?" She looked startled, and he said: "Any man who can listen to the first student of Copernicus picks up a lot of other things, too."

"I'm not surprised. One realm implies the other."

"You're one of those weird logicians, aren't you? One of those people who think about a world where there aren't noes or yeses. A Lewis Carroll kind of deal."

Ellen didn't anwer. The man continued: "You're probably

one of those perennial Ph.D. drop-outs, pretending to be someone else."

Ellen looked around to make sure no one was listening. "I
gave your chair a drink on the house. Will you bug off?"

"Well excuse me," said the man, waving a hand at the
chair. "I can see that my ramblings have bothered you." He got
up, folded the chair with solicitude, and put a ten dollar bill on
the bar. "The chair is grateful," he said. "It expresses its gratitude with money."

Malcolm was home, after all, drinking stale red wine from
a jelly glass. He hadn't found the infinitesimal particle, and had
discovered termites in the garage. "They're going to wreck the
house," he said.

"I doubt it," said Ellen. She opened her dresser and rummaged through it for a sweatshirt." I've had an odd evening. I
served a chair a drink."

"Let's get this straight. You served a drink to a chair?
Could the chair talk?"

"No. It belonged to some guy who thinks the chair was
the first student of Copernicus." She sighed and pulled off her
jeans. "Actually, the chair was beautiful. Delicate, like driftwood, with a pale mauve cover. I've never seen one like it.

"Maybe it's magic."

"What do you mean?"

"I mean maybe it was something else. Or someone else."
He smiled. "Maybe it transmogrified."

Sometimes Malcolm said things like that, and startled her
in a pleasant way. Like nine years ago, when he'd poured a glass
of wine and said—of the reflection in the bottle—*The vineyards at
Vincennes. They're in there....* She hadn't seen the vineyards at
Vincennes. She didn't even know if they existed. She'd simply
liked the way he said it. Now she didn't smile. She turned away
to put on her sweatshirt. "I don't think this chair is magic. I
think it's just a chair. Also I think the guy is crazy. No chair was
ever a student of Copernicus."

Malcolm put down his wine glass and turned off the light. Everything was black, except for silver stars on the ceiling, stars Malcolm bought at an environmental nature store. "You're losing your sense of humor," he said."Seriously. That Tap Room isn't good for you."

"I don't care."

"You don't care?"

"No, not particularly, not tonight. I mean would you care if you worked where people ordered drinks for chairs and I was always away looking at things no one can see? I think you wouldn't. This isn't a life."

"Well you can get a life. Finish the thesis and you'll be able to teach."

"I don't know if I'm interested anymore."

"Being interested isn't the point. Are you interested in the Tap Room?"

They'd had this conversation many times before, always in the dark, always in the evening. She turned away and felt Malcolm's flannel shirt against her back, then his arms around her.

"You don't have to work there, you know," he said. "You could take time off. Just finish it."

"Actually, I like the Tap Room."

"Really?"

"Yes. Something about the people. And the ginger crème brulée. Something about the crust. The way it breaks."

"Oh God," said Malcolm. "I'm going to sleep."

The next day, around noon, just before the artificial bells began to ring, she saw the same man on a hill, holding a pair of binoculars. He was wearing chinos and a melon-colored shirt, and the chair was next to him, looking serene among the wildflowers. The binoculars were poised in the man's hand so carefully, it occurred to her that he wasn't going to use them. Everything was a pose for the chair. For its terrible collision with Copernicus. For its peace and recuperation. He didn't see her, and she didn't wave.

Back at home she went to a room she called her study, and looked at piles of papers on an old daybed with an Indian bedspread. *When will you complete the task that you have set for yourself?* a former professor had written on a postcard from France. She turned it the other way, so all she could see was the picture.

When he came to the Tap Room that night, he didn't bring the chair. Ellen wondered if the chair had taken sick. Or perhaps the man hadn't wanted to risk Mo's gleeful malice. Without his asking she poured him the driest white they had, and he drank morosely. Thank God Mo wasn't there. She had no energy for running interference.

"How are you?" he asked.

"Fine. And you?"

"Burdened. It's a burden to carry around an inanimate object that is also so burdened and subject to ridicule. It's a burden to have to speak for something that can't speak for itself."

"Yes," she said. "I understand. Many of us do, in our own way...." She thought of her thesis which seemed to have existence only as a title: *Time and the Unicorn: The Logic of Imaginary Entities.* It couldn't speak for itself either.

"How liberal is this town?" the man asked. "I mean I never know what to call a person in your position. Are you a waitperson, a server? what?"

"This town is very liberal. And Ellen is just fine."

"I'm sorry. Are you really married?"

"Really. "

The bar was beginning to empty. She began to clean in earnest, wiping surfaces, washing glasses, blowing out candles.

"Ellen," said the man, musing over her name. "Ellen," he repeated, not talking to her, but about her.

"And what's your name?"

"Mark. Mark Van Der Geen."

"That's a long last name."

"You're right. But Mark is short."

She blew out the last candle and began to turn out lights. Mark waited for her, not pretending he wasn't, and they walked out together to the town green. It had just rained and a soft spring odor rose from the grass. "You're dying to know about me, aren't you? You think I'm some kind of nut, but still you're dying to know."

"Not exactly. And dying isn't the word for it. But to be honest there are two things I'm curious about: First, do you sleep with the chair? And second, do you sit on it?"

"Those are very unfair questions. They're personal and grossly intrusive. "

"I was only asking."

"Of course," he said, his voice turning to the same soft deference of the night before. "Anyway, I asked you to ask, and so I'll tell you. But can we walk?" She nodded, and they made their way across the green.

"In answer to your first question, I don't sleep with the chair at all. I mean, it's only a chair, and the reasons for its difficult history"—here he paused, looking sad—"have everything to do with its not being treated like a chair in the first place. So, no, I never sleep with it, even though I let it into my bedroom. If I did sleep with it, it might get confused—think it was a bed, or even a mistress. Can walk a little further?"

"Yes. Of course." Malcolm was working late again tonight. She wasn't expected anywhere.

"About your second question," he said, walking more quickly, "I sat on it only once, five years ago, when it became so desperate I had to remind it of its original purpose, which was to be a chair, and not the first student of Copernicus. So I did sit on it. But briefly."

"And what was it like?"

"Lonely. Unbearably lonely. I felt its confusion. Years and years of confusion."

"And did you sit on it again?"

"No. Never."

"Why not?"

"I can't explain. Something to do with respect."

They were walking towards the clapboard house that Mr. and Mrs. Lourdes had abandoned for Florida. They walked beyond the church, the general store, the path to the summer theater, navigating the dark, smelling the dense earth of pasture. On the front porch of the Lourdes' house, Mark paused, then opened the door. Inside were Oriental rugs, portraits of indistinct ancestors, enormous beveled mirrors. In the living room, among all these ancient things, was the slender, bone-white chair. An open book was on its lap and Mark had left on a lamp with a pink glass shade. She came close to the chair and saw that the book was a dictionary.

"You shouldn't be reading that. It's meant for the chair."

"You shouldn't have brought me here."

"Please. Don't be sarcastic. I've had a terrible day. Tomorrow we have to go home. The chair isn't happy here at all."

She looked at him, and saw he meant it. "I'm sorry," she said, "nothing should have a difficult life."

"Will you stay then? Stay for a nightcap."

"No. It wouldn't be fair to the chair." She was surprised she said it, and meant it. She began to move towards the door.

"Please stay."

"No. It wouldn't be a good idea." She paused at the door. "Good night," she said—half to him, half to the chair. And then, not quite able to leave, she added: "Maybe when you come back...."

"I don't think I'm coming back. So stay."

She was on the porch now, facing the stand of trees. Beyond the trees was the meadow, and beyond that was their house, where Malcolm might already be in bed, nursing a glass of cheap red wine. *I love you*, she wanted to say to Mark—recklessly, foolishly, not knowing if she meant it. Such words came from the dark—and it was from this place, surely, that she heard his inaudible answer.

THE WHITE COAT

Everything was cold and white and obvious in the far north of this country. The air achieved unusual clarity in the late afternoon, allowing one to view great distances. Even the snow implied patterns that might be decoded. Ellen Barlow felt no impediments or distractions as her children drank hot chocolate and her husband sipped brandy, nor was she startled by her failure to miss them. Here, in piles of snow, nothing happened in an ordinary way. People glided by on skis, as if touching the ground would reverse a promise. In cafes and shops, people talked softly—noise might release an avalanche. She remembered almost nothing of her life back home—the cramped little alcove where she did translations, their sprawling city apartment—everything vanished in this air of limitless depth.

Her family didn't share her amnesia. They talked about home as though a walk would get them a newspaper, and some imaginary switch would turn on television. The wooden farmhouse they'd rented had no electricity, so her children read books about time-warps and future civilizations, using clever book-flaps equipped with flashlights they'd ordered before they left. Her husband used one too, and at night she saw small pools of light where people were reading.

Ellen had wanted a house without electricity. She liked the kerosene lanterns—oddly shaped, with glass so thin they could be an extension of air. Even more, she liked candlelight. When everyone else was in bed and the fire turned to grey smoke, Ellen lit candles and read Montaigne. Montaigne was different by candlelight. She'd read Montaigne by day, long voluminous essays. Yet by this light, just one or two sentences were enough and could hold her for an entire night, like a prayer. She didn't remember them in the morning. Except for one. *It is a common enough occurrence to smile upon the misfortune of others.* This sentence trembled in the cold white air. Every night Ellen opened Montaigne at random and never found that sentence again, or anything else she'd read. Montaigne's essays became a book that never repeated itself. A book to be read by candlelight.

Unlike air in other countries—Hungary, or Russia—the air here had no history: No images of cabals, cafes, cigarette smoke. No sense of perilous adventure. The landscape veiled itself in white like a bride; you had to walk for a long time to find one blemish. Yet it was here, in this neutral country, that people were hauled out of barns and shot during the war. It was here that some of the most fatal raids had been carried out with precision. She knew this from books, and also heard it in the vague way people talked at the cafe: "My grandmother only sewed during the war. She embroidered very carefully, you know." Or: "We were traveling most of the time. My father imported coffee." Alibis were everywhere, as though war were still alive, yet the air was as clean as an abstract proof.

Before she'd left a friend told her that every winter he hid icicles in the hay in a farm in Canada, and every summer came back to find them. The hay had hidden the icicles and kept them from the heat. But the icicles had preserved themselves—he was sure of that. Ellen listened carefully, because she knew she was traveling to snow and wanted to immerse herself in another country. She wasn't interested in newly powdered snow, but in snow the country had preserved, ice from other centuries. Instead of skiing with her family, she went to the cafe in town, taking translations, and also books about the country's past. She intended to leave everything behind and start from the beginning.

Everyone here spoke English, and at first ignored her fluency. Eventually they stopped translating, yet nothing much was said. She felt like she was having conversations from a language primer. *Would you like more cream in your coffee? Yes, please. Today it's especially cold. I know—I wore an extra scarf.*

One woman in the cafe stood out from the others. She had long blond hair, an angular face, and read by herself at a table. Ellen recognized her as another translator, and soon they began to talk shop, using each other's language and laughing when things got jumbled. One day she asked this woman, whose name was Anna, what her parents had done during the war. Anna looked insulted and said: "I wasn't born yet."

"Of course you hadn't. But your parents were."

Anna shrugged. "Why are you so interested?"

"I'm not sure, exactly. I came here to be distracted."

"From what?"

"From everything at home. Why else would you go on vacation?"

Anna looked outside at the fields of snow that could blind you. "This is an easy place to be distracted," she said. "You shouldn't have to think about war for that to happen." She smiled and went back to her books.

Ellen supposed that Anna was right. She seemed to have forgotten almost everything, except her children and husband— and even they seemed distant, seen through wavy glass. The only thing she remembered about home was an exhibit of clothes she'd seen in a museum a week before they left. In particular, she remembered a mannequin wearing an ermine coat with white boots and white stockings. The catalogue explained that such coats were worn in Europe over a hundred years ago and called 'camouflage coats,' because whenever women wore them, they faded into the snow. She remembered the coat often, along with the phrase from Montaigne: *It is a common*

158

enough occurrence to smile upon the misfortune of others. Ellen wondered to what purpose these women had wanted to seem to disappear. Perhaps to surprise. Perhaps on a whim.

While she read in the evenings, her husband snored above her in a quaint wooden loft. They were on a long vacation because they were thinking of divorce, and once wrote in their marriage contract that if either of them wanted divorce, they would spend at least three weeks together *getting away from it all*. When they'd written the contract, they had no children, and imagined getting away from it all would mean going on a trek to Nepal. They also imagined that only one of them would want a divorce: As it turned out, both of them did, so her husband said: "We should multiply our doubts by two, and go away for six weeks. With the kids." The fact that he said *doubt* was telling, Ellen thought: it meant that he didn't want a divorce after all, and was only matching her feelings to save face. Sometimes, after reading Montaigne, she slipped into the bedroom and lay next to him. In sleep, he forgot he was angry with her. He held her in the dark, and pulled her against him, spoon fashion.

During the day, her husband and children stayed on the slopes skiing and having hot chocolate and warm soup in mountain inns. Ellen skied for hours on flat country, worked on dull technical translations, and read foreign detective novels that were full of umlauts. One day she saw Anna in the cafe and said: "I saw a coat in New York that made me think of a perfect way to cover-up a crime." Anna looked blank. "I'm sure you know about them," she continued: "Women wore coats like that over a hundred years ago in Europe. They were called 'camouflage coats' because they made these women disappear in the snow. Does it ring a bell?"

A lid fell from Anna's eyes. She put her translations aside and stared at the impenetrable white fields. "My great-grandmother had the most amazing clothes," she said. "And it was the time of the white coats, so she had one, too." The phrase *time of the white coats* made it sound as though the coats were like Leningrad's white nights—an extravagance, an intoxication.

"Do you still have it?" Ellen asked.

"Yes," Anna said. "It's been in the family for years." She paused, hesitated, closed her book: "Would you like to come over to my house and see the coat?"

She could not believe she would be allowed to come inside this house with a pointed roof and sloping door. People were friendly when they talked, but never brought strangers home, and the moment she entered the house, she knew why: Outside the air was clear. Inside the air was thick, old, stale, and redolent with human arguments. Soup brewed on the stove. Books obscured a long pine table.

"Forgive the mess," said Anna. "I live alone and do more than one translation at a time." Before she had time to tell her that a mess was no problem, Anna motioned her upstairs. "I turned to translations when my husband left," she said. "My family had no money after the war. And my husband lied to me about his. Or—to put it more politely—he used his money for other things. I had to sell everything except this coat." Anna was speaking English now—fluently, like everybody else—except in her case, it seemed like it was really her own language. Anna led her to the second floor, walking quickly past rooms that once had belonged to children—Ellen saw dressers with decals of wooden shoes, stuffed bears piled on beds. Anna led her up another flight of stairs, and opened the door to an attic. The musty smell brought back her grandmother's attic in Indiana, a cavernous room with dampness everywhere. This attic was also large. Eight dormer windows looked out on endless snow. "I've often thought of converting this," Anna said. "I like the idea of working under the eaves."

Unlike her grandmother's attic, this room was well ordered. There were trunks of sturdy wood with brass handles, and oak bookcases filled with books—some so large they lay on their sides. There was also a pine armoire, which Anna opened with a huge key, trustingly left in its lock. She brought something out that looked like a corpse—something in the shape of a woman wrapped many times over in white linen. Anna unwrapped the cloth and beneath it—improbably, because everything here was archaic—were layers of plastic. She unwrapped those, too, and suddenly Ellen saw a white ermine coat more perfect than the coat in the museum. It was made of pure white fur and had matching buttons. The ermine was invisibly stitched, so the skirt fell in folds. The whole coat looked like snow. Ellen forgot she was repelled by coats made from animals. She wanted to stroke the coat, pet it.

Anna let her touch the coat, but briefly. She opened a shallow door that concealed another door which led to a large windowless room. This room had a second door that led to a corridor that was narrow and claustrophobic. They walked down the corridor, Anna holding the coat, until they reached a door that led outside to the snow. "My grandparents kept people here during the war," Anna said. "It was part of their job. But that isn't the point. This"—and she laid the coat carefully on the ground—"is the point. Look: You can hardly see it. It belonged to my great-grandmother and my grandparents used it to smuggle people here. You can't imagine how many people wore this coat when they walked through the woods. Men so large they had to wear white suits underneath because they couldn't button the buttons. Children so short they trailed the coat in the snow and stumbled. My grandparents had to bring everybody one at a time. I was told it was very tedious.

"In any case, there was something uncanny about this coat. People wearing it were always concealed. It didn't matter who saw the people accompanying them. It didn't matter who stopped to ask questions. Our family came to believe the coat had magical properties. I promised my mother I'd save it in case of another war." Anna spoke matter-of-factly. Then she looked around, as if she'd committed a transgression. "I've kept this coat outside long enough," she said. "We should go in now."

Anna picked up the invisible coat and its shape reassembled in her arms. They went in by the back door, and she pulled out a copy of *Mansfield Park* from a kitchen shelf. "You can read this," she said to Ellen. "I'll put the coat back in its wrappings."

Ellen picked up *Mansfield Park*, feeling cheated. She wanted to spend more time with the coat.

Anna was upstairs now. She could hear her trudge on the creaking wood, and realized she didn't even know her last name. She looked on the table for signs, but all she saw was a language she couldn't decipher. Turkish, she supposed. The clock ticked. Soup simmered on the stove. For a while she heard soft sounds in the attic. Then Anna came downstairs and offered her tea.

"I'd prefer coffee," she said.

"So would I," said Anna. "Tea just always seems like the right thing to serve people, doesn't it?"

Anna was speaking in many languages at once. Or perhaps it was no longer possible for Ellen to distinguish her own language from the language of the country. She didn't know. Her ears felt open, alien. As Anna made coffee she heard every sound—the clock, the soup, and an uzi-sound made by a snow-laden tree. She even imagined she heard the coat, settling back in its layers, adjusting to a life of hiding beneath white cloth, a life of *waiting just in case*. She wanted the coat very much. But she was not a criminal. If just once, she thought, I could borrow the coat. If just once I could wear it in the snow. Of course she didn't ask. She sat while Anna brought strong coffee in cream-colored bowls, and drank with her silently. Finally she heard herself say, "What a coincidence that I mentioned that coat."

"What coat?" said Anna.

"The coat in the museum."

"Yes," said Anna, "a coincidence indeed." It was clear she didn't think it was, but found it a mere accident—and not a very interesting one. Anna's indifference drove her on.

"I've been thinking of that coat constantly, ever since I saw the exhibit. In fact, besides Montaigne, it's all I think about."

"Oh?" said Anna. "And have you been here long?"

"Four weeks," she said. "We're staying here for two more."

"In that case," said Anna, "you won't forget the coat. If you were staying here longer, I'd imagine you might. There's something about this place: people don't remember much."

"And yet they talk about the war all the time."

"Well, in a sense. But obliquely."

She now wanted to wear the coat very badly. But she wasn't used to asking for things at all. Like cautious climbers in the Himalayas, she always chose indirect, inelegant routes.

"How were its properties discovered?" she asked.

"What properties?" said Anna.

"The extraordinary properties of the coat," she answered.

Anna stretched, looked at her translations. Since showing her the coat, she'd assumed the most laconic manner, as if they didn't have anything to talk about. "Well, in one sense," she said, as though she were bored, "it only became obvious after the fact. I mean people had worn it and no one had been caught, and pretty soon my grandmother began to wonder why."

Anna looked at her translations again, but Ellen—the seeker of the coat, the believer in totems—waited. She'd learned to be silent in a way that was aggressively loud and used that power now. Outside, trees creaked in a rising wind. Soon her husband and children would be coming home from the slopes. She waited.

At last Anna sighed and said with some reluctance: "Well, the coat always brought luck to anyone who wore it. But there was one particular time when a man who was very valuable in this...in this whole enterprise...was in great danger of his life, and had to be hidden here. He was an eccentric man and also very large. There was another thing, too: he had a strange medical problem, which was that he fell asleep at unpredictable moments. A kind of..." here she groped, "intermittent narcolepsy. Yes. I guess that would be the only way to describe it: *intermittent narcolepsy*. In any case, it was clear he had to be hidden, and since the coat had been lucky for other people, there was no question that he had to wear it. But he was so large! My grandmother found an enormous white suit and decided the man would wear the coat over the suit. And then my grandfather decided not to escort the man himself, but made my aunt—she was sixteen and looked very innocent—be the one to escort him. It was a tradition that whoever went to escort the new fugitive wore the coat for protection on the way, so my aunt wore the coat to the farmhouse where the man was staying. Then she took off the coat, got out the suit and began to try to dress him. This man—as I said, he was very large—kept falling asleep. Two men had to help, and finally my aunt said: 'I thought he didn't fall asleep that way. I thought he could *make* himself be awake.' 'He's never fallen asleep like this before,' said one of the men, 'maybe he's nervous.' 'Nervous or not,' said my aunt, 'I'm not sure taking him anywhere is a good idea.' One of the men held a gun to her head. The other fell on his knees and began to cry. 'We have no choice,' he said. 'This man is an expert forger and has connections in the diamond business.'

"My aunt couldn't argue with them, so they set out in the woods through the snow. At first the air revived the man. Maybe you've noticed this about the air here. It has a way of pushing people forward and not letting them lean against it. But half way to the farmhouse, the man fell asleep. He fell asleep standing up, like a tree. And there was nothing my aunt could do about it."

Anna stopped and poured more coffee for both of them. "You have to understand there were spies everywhere. And they also were like trees. They even hid in trees and came out of them. Someone came out of one right then—a farmer named Lars with connections to the secret police. He had this way about him so you couldn't even think to mention how odd it seemed that he'd come out of a tree. He and my aunt talked about the weather and the price of beer at a local tavern and all the time they talked, this enormous man was not only sleeping but snoring loudly. God knows what Lars thought the sound was. Maybe he thought my aunt was"—Anna stopped, decided upon a word—"*farting*. I have no idea. I only know that after a while he said good-bye and my aunt brought this man back to the house. Not that it was easy. My grandparents already had five people in that room, and this man was a total boor. Finally they sent him to England. But if Lars had known about him, he would have turned him in because Lars turned in everybody, including children and old people. That's when my family decided the coat was extraordinary. Or—who knows?—maybe the coat was just heroic. Maybe certain objects, like people, just did what they had to do in the war." Anna leaned on the table, as if the story exhausted her.

"You mean no one has worn the coat since the war?"

"No. Why would they?"

"To test the magic."

"Oh, our family wasn't like that. The coat worked. That's all that mattered. And when we didn't need it any more, we put it away. Besides, maybe if we tested it, the coat would sense our doubts. Then it would be insulted and deny us protection when we needed it."

Ellen saw her move, and decided to take it. "I would love to wear it," she said. "Just once. In the snow."

Anna looked startled. Her eyes, clear with memory, became opaque. "Really? Why?"

"Not to be seen!"

"But you have no reason."

"There are lots of reasons not to be seen. Lots of reasons besides wars." She thought of trying to explain something—about her husband, Montaigne, candlelight.

Anna held up a hand. "I'm sorry, but I can't let you. This coat is for serious service, not for whims." Her voice softened, and her eyes looked sad. "I didn't mean you wanted to wear it on a whim," she said. "I just meant that this is a coat for emergencies."

"Oh, but this is an emergency. I would like, just once, to disappear."

"I don't understand."

"You wouldn't want to."

Anna reconsidered. "How long do you need?"

"Only five minutes. I just want to walk outside and stand in the snow near your house. Maybe you could tell me if you could see me. Or—if you didn't want to do that"—suddenly she felt accommodating—"maybe I could find out for myself."

Anna lit a cigarette and took a long drag on it. "What the hell," she said, using a vernacular she'd never used and seeming to address a row of uncles who wagged their fingers, two grandmothers who might faint—as well as a battalion of fugitives. "You wait here," she said, pushing back her chair. "No stranger ever took the coat from the attic. That was the family's job."

She pushed back her chair and began the long walk upstairs. She was gone so long, Ellen wondered if Anna had decided to trick her, then remembered that the coat must be unwrapped from its casing. The fact that she wouldn't see Anna unwrap the coat disappointed her. The unveiling was part of the coat, an essential piece of its history. Eventually she heard footsteps, and Anna came downstairs wearing the coat. She could see her clearly and was disappointed.

"Don't worry," said Anna, catching her disappointment. "The camouflage only works outdoors, in the snow."

She then showed her white leather boots, white stockings, white gloves and a white fur hat. "We had all kinds of accessories in different sizes. My family wasn't taking chances. I thought these might fit."

Everything fit perfectly. Ellen felt unremarkable. There was a mirror in the hall, and when she saw herself in it she thought of the mannequin in the museum. The mannequin's porcelain face looked small and apologetic, just like her face did now.

"Don't worry," said Anna. "If it works, it's only in the snow." She opened the door and motioned for her to leave. "Go for a walk. But not for long. I don't want to take advantage of what this coat has given us."

Ellen went outside and everything was the same. She'd imagined the air would be a triumphant extension of the coat, and therefore an extension of herself. Instead, it was merely cold. There was no memory in the air, yet nothing was concealed. She could hear her own breath, the labor of her footsteps. She walked down a path, hoping that someone would show up and not notice her. No one came. She deviated from that path, hoping to meet someone coming from the slopes, a grandson of Lars, the farmer, even her husband and children. This path was also deserted, so she had to be content to walk alone, wearing the coat. It was soft, and made her feel at one with the snow, as though she and the snow were a new and singular element. When she returned, Anna answered the door solemnly. "That coat hasn't failed us," she said. "I wasn't able to see you."

"Are you sure?"

"Yes. All I could see was snow."

For a moment Ellen felt betrayed and realized she'd wanted Anna to knock loudly at the window, and cry with great excitement, "Guess what! I can't see you!" Anna seemed to guess this. Her face signaled that the coat meant serious disappearance, and not a game of hide-and-seek. Ellen thanked Anna profusely, offered to go upstairs and help return the coat to its labyrinthine wrappings.

"No thank you," Anna said. "It was always a tradition that someone in the family would do that. In fact," and here she looked away, "we are very respectful of the coat. We even thank it." She reached out and shook Ellen's hand. "I think I should thank you, too. I never got to help anyone with this coat. I only heard about it. In a sense, you helped me understand something."

After Ellen wore the coat, everything was the same. She still felt distant from her children and read Montaigne by candlelight. She still ignored her husband in the evenings.

"What are we doing here?" she asked him once.

"Figuring out options," he answered.

"What options?" she asked. He mumbled something about negotiating, but she'd already opened Montaigne, whom

167

she was no longer reading in French since Anna had loaned her a copy. In this new language, Montaigne's voice had fewer arcs and curlicues. Still, by candlelight, he floated over centuries.

At the corner store she and Anna sometimes stood close to each other while people ordered sugar, flour, milk. A new intimacy arose between them. She showed Anna a book by a Polish writer she admired. Anna lent her the copy of Montaigne. Sometimes one bought the other coffee, or an extra roll. Neither mentioned the coat. Nor did Ellen think of it alone. Maybe Anna was right about memory disappearing here. Or maybe camouflage conceals itself—so in a sense, it never happened.

A week before they were going to leave, she decided to return Anna's copy of Montaigne. Anna was at the kitchen table, working on the same translation. More soup was bubbling on the stove.

"Keep it," Anna said, gesturing at the book, "I'll never read it again."

"Are you sure?"

"Absolutely," Anna extended her hand. "I'll see you in the cafe, yes? We won't say good-bye."

"No, of course not. I still have a week."

Ellen walked out the door, feeling she had no country, no history of her own. She was a citizen of this country, sometime during the war, and on a mission, a mission for someone in trouble. She had guns, cyanide, was prepared to do something reckless. The mission was difficult, and involved bringing secret news. She imagined that she accomplished her mission, and came back to find the small wooden farmhouse in ruins. War had broken out. Her family was gone. Life, as she knew it, was over. As she came towards her farmhouse, she became convinced that what she was imagining was true in spite of the fact that there was no war, and she wasn't on any kind of mission, except to save herself and read Montaigne. What relief when she walked up the path to the wooden house, and her children

168

opened the door, and raced out to meet her. What relief when they tumbled against her in warm rough sweaters, arguing for attention. They were real, absolute, bony. And they carried with them their own mysterious complications, their own ineffable dreams. "You were out for much too long," her five-year-old scolded. "Much longer than you'd ever let *us* be." She stamped her foot in the snow. The powdery dust flew around them.

SLEEPING IN VELVET

How long had they both been sleeping in velvet? A year? Two? They didn't know. She wore a faded black tiered skirt, and a crimson blouse with frilled cuffs, open at the neck, always open, and he wore a long brown coat, very thin, very long, it could have been a bathrobe—maybe it was, even—but he insisted on calling it a coat and sometimes he wore it to the opera. They didn't sleep in the plush velvet of Fifth Avenue stores, but in the ratty, tawdry velvet of vintage outlets. It was velvet where the black looked brown and the fabric was piebald and the brown had a ghostly yellow cast. They had other velvet clothes, too—a smoking jacket, a long black dress, hats, scarves, belts, bags—but they always wore the same velvet things to bed. He never wore anything on his feet. She often wore cream-colored, surprisingly thick running socks, bunched low. He thought she looked like a dancer who had fallen into bed. And she thought he looked like a 19th century dandy, not at all the way he looked during the day when he waited on tables. Sometimes they made up stories about each other. Risqué stories that talked about lives in different centuries. But only sometimes. Most of the time, they just slept together wearing velvet. They had a down comforter, too—a luxury, not second-hand.

It was a friend who caught them sleeping in velvet. They'd lent him a key when he stopped over on his way to England. He'd never given it back and when he returned he let himself into their apartment at one in the morning and found them sleeping. The comforter was pulled low, and the velvets blended into each other, creating odd curves, intricate boundaries. "My God!" he said, and they woke up and looked at him calmly, like children in a picture. "Do you always sleep that way?" he asked. "Yes, I guess so," one of them said. "It isn't as though we ever thought about it. But yes, I guess we do." She sat up in bed, and touched her soft, crimson sleeve. So opulent. So Edwardian. And when the friend saw her touch the sleeve, he knew they were lying. Of course they had decided to sleep in velvet on purpose. It was clear. They knew what they were doing.

Soon they were in the kitchen, sitting around a dark round table with the white toaster and salt and pepper shakers in the shape of wind mills. It was a small table. The three of them had to sit close, and she offered him rolls and bitter coffee. *Generous*, he thought as he ate, *they are so generous....* And all at once he told them he wanted to paint them sleeping in velvet. They agreed. "Why not? It's a habit, nothing that we really think about.... And we don't have to do anything except sleep, do we?" "No," he answered. "All you have to do is sleep." When they left to go to their jobs, the friend lay down in their bed, which felt ordinary in his clothes. For a moment he wanted to look through their closet, find the brown velvet robe, maybe even the skirt, and put them on. He restrained himself.

That night he set up a canvas in their room while the two of them got into bed. "Don't work too hard," they said, before going to sleep. "Don't worry," he answered, "I won't." But it was a long night for him, getting it just right, the tawdry feel of the fabric between the chasms, passageways, pockets of velvet he couldn't see. And the electric moments when the velvets touched. He used a combination of oil pastels and charcoal, and the more he smudged and worked and colored, the more the whole scene was imprinted in his body. "You've made it all up," they said when they looked at his picture in the morning. "All we ever did was sleep." Yet even as they spoke, they had the self-satisfaction of cats who leap without exercising, cats who are elegantly furred. "You made it all up," they said again, shrugging. But it was clear they knew he hadn't. And he knew they liked the picture.

Soon they were in the kitchen again, huddling around the small round table. The three of them had to sit close, and she was solicitous, making him special pieces of toast from old stale bread—hard ryes, sweet bits of challah, pumpernickel. "We save it all," she said, "because we aren't rich."

The friend was quiet, morose. He'd spent all night drenching himself in velvet, and all he had was a picture. He was thinking of giving it to them without asking for money because he knew they wanted it. Yet, out of some perversity, he lugged it from their apartment, bumping down the four flights of stairs into the freezing cold. But when he saw how it was snowing, he came back, knocking quickly and letting himself in with the same key. "I can't take this out," he said, "it will get ruined. You keep it." "Oh no," they said. "You could sell it. Wait and see. Really. You'll be surprised."

It was Sunday and very cold. They were already back in bed, close in each other's arms, almost sleeping. "Get into bed with us," they said. "Not with your clothes. Just you." He put the picture against the wall, took off his clothes and got into bed between them. The velvet reached over him and around him like a bridge, and he was enclosed in it, encased in it, and knew what it was like to be each one of them separately, and the two of them together, and something else, too—velvet. That's what velvet does, he thought, it makes you feel like what it is. He didn't say this though. He'd been up all night, was tired, and knew he could never sell the picture. "Just love me," he said. "We do," they answered.

THE MAP MAKER

ONTENTS

Where got I that truth?
Out of a medium's mouth,
Out of nothing it came,
Out of the forest loam,
Out of the dark night where lay
The crowns of Ninevah.

from *Fragments,*
by William Butler Yeats

for Elie and Martha
—with love and gratitude

I

Ninevah

The map was of ancient Asia, purchased by my grandfather in a second-hand bookstore on 4th Avenue in New York.
It was part of my grandfather's search for a real, definitive tome,
and although the map wasn't a book, it was imposing enough
to stand for one. This map was made in the 18th century. The
countries were inked with dark green and purple-veined as
veins would be, if connected to the earth. The map had a com-
pass of the four directions placed in the middle of the ocean.
This added to the sense that the terrain might not exist in ordinary time. My grandfather's search for old maps and rare books
was fueled by his decision to leave his *shtetl* in Rumania and
become a doctor in New York. This made him the first son who
didn't write commentaries on the Torah, a tradition begun by
his ancestors hundreds of years ago. Perhaps for this reason he
searched for documents that were old, books from the beginning of history. In addition to the map, he bought an Assyrian
parchment with blurred writing. No one knew how old it was.

The map of Asia was as nomadic as its former inhabitants.
First it hung in my grandfather's office in New York. When he
remarried and his second wife didn't like it, he gave it to us so
it could live in our tiny apartment in Kansas. Sometimes it hung
in my father's study, a small, mysterious alcove, where he wrote
his books on Renaissance architecture. Sometimes it was in my
parents' bedroom, a large, cavernous room where my mother
devoted the first part of her day to sleeping. Wherever the map
happened to be, I always looked at it, particularly at the

pictures. There was a nude woman pouring water from a wedge-shaped pitcher and a Christ-like figure offering a cup, a saucer, and a tiny map. I was embarrassed by the woman's nudity, but fascinated by her pitcher. Its water spilled in two directions, one right into the sea.

At night when I couldn't sleep, I'd sometimes contrive to kick my father out of bed and my mother would always tell me the story about the man who had made the map. Her voice was soft in the dark—not harsh, the way it often was during the day—and she told me the story as though she'd seen this man from a secret, careful distance. He was already an old man when he decided to make the map, she said, but vigorous and strong. He wore a leather jerkin, seven-league boots, and carried a large staff so he could climb valleys and mountains. Mapmakers were rare in those days, my mother told me. Whenever he arrived in villages people came to greet him. They fed him dark bread with strong crusts, pitchers of wine, and hot, sweet porridge. For this reason, he was nearly eighty by the time he reached Asia and when he came home, he was almost a hundred. "The map we have is the map of Asia," she said. "He made it in 1716, and it's one of the oldest in the world."

It wasn't one of the oldest maps of the world. I found this out when I studied geography in college; but for a while I believed my mother and bragged to my classmates.

My mother told me the story as if remembering a past that was real. This was a past that no one left, changed, or entered— yet my mother had been in it, I was sure of that, just as I was sure she had met the mapmaker.

"Did you see him?" I asked her.

"Of course not," she said. I was sure she was lying.

Even though the map was of Asia, I decided that my mother had lived in Europe, because that was the part of his journey she talked about the most. Peasants in ruffled blouses danced for the mapmaker. Dark braided bread appeared on tables for him. And Asia—his ultimate destination—was shrouded. If I asked her to tell me about countries he'd visited in Asia, she said they weren't the point. The point was his journey, particularly in his boat, where the four direction were as variable as the winds.

"What did he do on the boat?"

"He wrote letters to people at home. Of course it was a long time before he landed and could find someone who could send them. Sometimes the letters got lost."

I knew—by some ineffable transmission of the air—that in my mother's mind the mapmaker and my grandfather were the same person. My grandfather—her father—was a doctor with expensive clothes, and a penchant for red carnations in his lapel. When he came to visit in Kansas, with his wild woolly hair and heavy woolen coat, he looked like no one else on those long flat streets. He spoke with the oddest accent I'd ever heard, as if he were talking through water, and he had an enormous lump on his nose—the result of being burned when he ran into a samovar at age three. As my mother talked, it was my grandfather I imagined in the dark. His boots were green and purple, just like the colors of the map; however his coat was black, like the coat he wore when he came to visit us. I saw him with peasants in the mountains, leaning close to their ruffled blouses. His hair was frizzy and white. The lump on his nose was large.

When I became too old to sleep with my mother, I grew more curious about Asia. My mother had referred to people who migrated across the desert called Yemenites. She said the mapmaker had nothing to do with them, indeed, he found them crazy because they were part of a religious sect. I was curious but knew better than to ask more. My parents—one the daughter of a former Hassid, the other the son of a Presbyterian theologian—were serious, careful Marxists and it wasn't part of their program to discuss anything holy. I looked up *Yemenite* in

179

my World Encyclopedia, and saw a picture of someone in dark robes, standing alone on a desert. I went back to the map. looked at it carefully and saw no signs of Yemenites.

Everything on the map was written in Latin. Its name—*Asia Cum Omnibus Imperius*—and the ancient wonders of the world: Terra Sancta, which I later learned was Jerusalem, and Muro Extra—China's Great Wall. In the country of Assyria, I noticed a large city surrounded by trees. This city was drawn in gold, its name was Ninevah, and it had a book in its center. I looked at it more closely, saw the words *Lector Benevol* on the book, wrote them down and took them to my mother. She was bending over the stove, taking out a braided bread, much like breads the mapmaker had been given.

My mother looked stern, as though I'd been going through her chest of drawers without permission. "Where did you read those words?" she asked.

"On the map. The map of Asia."

"That means Gentle Reader," said my mother, who had studied Latin in high school.

"Did the map maker go there?"

"Where?"

"To Ninevah. That place with the book."

"Of course. He went everywhere." My mother set the bread on top of the table and dusted it with flour. "Ninevah was the last place he stopped," she said. "And then, after that, he went back home. First he had to go in that awful boat, and then he walked over mountains and valleys until he came to his village. The children of the village were happy to see him."

It was growing dark, late winter dusk. I saw the mapmaker coming home to a cottage I'd seen in a Grimm's fairy tale book—a cottage with a thatched and sloping roof. Beyond the cottage I could see the vast, limitless outlines of some deeper, urgent darkness.

"Where was Ninevah?" I asked.

"Right where you saw it on the map."

"And now?"

"And now it's nowhere."

At night when I couldn't sleep, I sometimes snuck to my father's study and looked at the country of Ninevah. It seemed to be drawn differently from other parts of the map, as if another country were hiding beneath it.

DIME STORE

Twice a year my grandfather came to visit us in Kansas. Since he needed luxuries we couldn't provide—showers with rough towels, impeccable room service—he always stayed at the glamorous Wilmore Hotel.

"My father needs a board in his bed," my mother announced to some invisible person on the phone, while she tapped cigarette ashes on the floor. "He has a very bad back and needs a good board."

Invariably, someone at the Wilmore told my mother there was no way they would drag an enormous board to the tenth or eleventh floor of their hotel. My mother's voice grew more severe.

"A board," she repeated. "A good *thick* board. Otherwise he simply won't stay. What? That's ridiculous. Of course you can get someone to find one."

On the day of this particular argument, my mother was in my father's study, sitting on the daybed. I was on the floor, playing with a snowstorm paperweight. *What are you doing?* she mouthed to me.

"Nothing," I said. "Just playing." In fact, I was thinking that the snow looked like cottage cheese and wishing I could break the paperweight to find out.

"A board," my mother repeated, speaking back to the phone. "A very good thick board. I'm sorry. We insist. He's from New York."

My grandfather's picture was on my father's desk. He was

reading a book and I could see his white frizzy hair and the lump on his nose. When he'd first told me about running into the samovar, I imagined a three-year-old with a wreath of frizzy white hair wearing a navy-blue, double-breasted suit, decorated with a carnation. I imagined him this way now.

"Well that's settled," said my mother, putting down the phone. "You'd think they'd never heard of a bad back before." She took a drag on her cigarette, and fluffed up the sleeves of her green housecoat. "The things that man doesn't do for people. The lengths to which he will go." I continued to play with the paperweight. She grew annoyed with my indifference. "His generosity," she added testily. "Everyone is indebted to him." She meant that sometimes he made house calls in tenements, delivered children on kitchen tables, helped soldiers get shots for the Spanish Civil War. She also meant he gave us money.

"You'll stay with him for a night," she said to me. "The Wilmore is marvelous."

"What?" I shook the paperweight harder. The snowman disappeared.

"In the Wilmore. You can stay overnight with him. You'll be his guest."

My grandfather arrived at seven o'clock that night, and within hours I was in at the Wilmore, being given a bath that frightened me, as he splashed water and screamed "Get down! Get down!" Since I wasn't really able to go anywhere, I didn't know if he wanted me to dive under the water or lean back against the slippery back of the gleaming white tub. I was much too old to be given a bath, and much too old to be dried, but I'd always been told never to say no.

When he led me to the bedroom, I was relieved that both beds were arranged end to end—mine above his. There was so little space between them, it seemed to me they looked like one bed meant for a very long person. My bed seemed hard. I wondered if it had a board.

For a long time I lay in bed, and the darkness smelled thick with oil my grandfather had used, although I wasn't sure if it were on his body or mine. He was the mapmaker, I knew that for certain—the man who'd walked in seven league boots and been fed sweet wine and braided bread. He was the map-maker, taking time off.

The night was not exotic like any of the countries my mother had described. Downtown Lawrence was thick and ordinary. I fell asleep to my mother intoning... *and so he walked all over the land in his enormous seven league boots....* I woke up at dawn.

In story books I sometimes read about people who woke up in the morning and couldn't remember where they were. I longed to have this experience, but that morning, like all others, I remembered where I was. My grandfather was lying on his bed on top of the covers: I could see the froth of his hair like a large white shrub. I could even look through it, just as I could look through brambles, and through the tangle, I saw him pull his penis out of his pajamas and push it and pull it until white whale's milk spurted into the air. Afterwards the grey dawn began to pull and pull at the walls, like taffy. At last there was no air left at all.

When my first-grade teacher, Mrs. Ryan, found four boys and one girl in a state of disarray behind coats in the cloak-room, she told us that grown-ups do not play with themselves, and indeed if we wanted to be grown-ups we would do the same. Of course we did not want to be grown-ups and ignored her. However, in this strange airless room, Mrs. Ryan's word became law and once more my grandfather became an enormous naked child, running towards a samovar. His penis began to look like the spout of the samovar. I decided that he deserved to be burned.

At breakfast, I told my grandfather what I had seen. Perhaps if I could have eaten I wouldn't have bothered to tell him, but the orange juice was viscous, and the toast as rough as a man's cheek.

"You sly little girl," he said, when I finished. "You sly, sly little girl."

The dining room of the Wilmore was across the street from the public library. I could see its carved oak doors, and wished I could open them, talk to the librarian and get my quota of four books for the week. Instead, I sat quietly, contemplating the meaning of *sly*, and finally said to my grandfather: "I want you to buy me a present."

"A present?"

"Yes. A present."

My grandfather didn't argue. In fact, he nodded, as though responding to an ancient, familiar imperative. Outside, the midwest became a place the mapmaker couldn't chart, no matter how many peasants he waved to—a land of tired pink houses, plastic bobby pins, dime stores. I guided my grandfather through Woolworth's, past blue binders, strawberry-colored rulers, globes of countries I never wanted to see. His dark wool coat was larger there—like a topiary I'd seen in a mansion.

My grandfather followed me to a glass counter filled with ribbon candy and plastic wind-up toys. I pointed to a man in a black tuxedo hugging a woman in a flamingo-colored evening dress.

"I want that," I said. "I want you to buy that for me."

My grandfather nodded. An exceedingly uncomfortable nod. Followed by the phrase: "The young lady wants to see that."

The clerk put the man and woman on top of the counter and they spun around and around. As soon as we got to my parents' apartment, I put them on our mahogany dining room table and made them dance until they fell, since not even a key could unwind them.

SANDRA GREENAWAY

Sandra Greenaway's mother was the head housekeeper at the Wilmore, and this meant that she and her mother had two suites to themselves with a kitchen. Sandra was embarrassed that her mother was the housekeeper at the Wilmore. She was so embarrassed that twice a year she invited five second-grade girls to her private suite for tea, during which she spoke in a fake English accent. My mother said that maybe Sandra was a relative of Kate Greenaway, the artist who drew women in empire dresses, but I never mentioned this to Sandra, because I didn't want her to know that my mother speculated about things like that, nor did I want her to know that I romanticized her surroundings.

The first time Sandra invited us over to tea, I imagined something exotic was going to happen, even if it was sad. Maybe we would explore the Wilmore and get locked in an upstairs room. Maybe we'd walk into the picture of a castle in the lobby and disappear. Nothing happened at all: Sandra poured bland Earl Grey, served us something called cream crackers, talked in her fake English accent, and we all went home. This was before I'd gone to the Wilmore with my grandfather, so I wished that I could live there.

About a month after my grandfather left, I asked Sandra to come over for tea. I was ashamed our apartment was small and drab, yet felt compelled to let her see it. Since my mother was—according to standards of Kansas—the sort of woman who "let things go," our green rug was usually dirty, our brown couch flecked with lint, and the floor covered with newspapers. Yet the moment Sandra walked inside, I realized she envied me

186

because my mother didn't have to be a housekeeper so we could live here. It wasn't in anything she said. Just a sadness in her eyes, an intake of breath.

"Come in," I said, faking an English accent.

My mother let us use her best China teacups and we drank the same bland Earl Grey tea Sandra had served. Instead of cream crackers we ate Mallomars, which Sandra said were "jolly good." While we ate, we sat at the small white table in my room, facing the ribbon of alleys—a place where I hid when my parents fought, and kept an old attaché case of my father's filled with old draperies, in case I had to run away from home. However, Sandra said, verging in on her English accent:

"What a nice desk! I should like to have one."

"It's not a desk. It's a table."

"Well. A table then," said Sandra.

"But you have one, don't you?"

"Yes. But not my own." Sandra looked out at the ribbon of alleys.

"You're lucky to visit the Wilmore," she said. "I have to live there, but you get to eat in the dining room."

"I've never eaten in the dining room."

"But I saw you. You got to stay with that man—the man with the white hair."

"Why didn't you come in and say hi if you saw me?"

"I'm not allowed in the dining room."

I thought of the two narrow beds and my grandfather's penis haloed by frizzy white hair—an image that would appear for years, each time I heard a dirty joke, or even considered the word. I wondered if Sandra's mother had cleaned that room and seen his milk on the sheets. I wondered if she and her mother had heard my grandfather giving me a bath.

"It was only one night. Besides, breakfast wasn't much fun."

"Why not?" said Sandra in her prim, self-conscious way.

"Because. There were boogers in the orange juice."

There hadn't been boogers in the orange juice—but Sandra laughed in a way I'd never seen her laugh and I told myself that I could fool anybody I wanted to.

"Were there *really?*" she kept saying. "Were there *really?*"

"Yes," I said. "And more. You could hear them blowing their noses in the kitchen."

"Oh no," said Sandra.

"Oh yes. The whole place was full of blowing their noses."

On the way out Sandra stopped at my father's study and looked at the map of Asia.

"What's that?"

"A map, silly."

"I know. But of what?"

"Asia."

"But it's *green*. And *purple*. I thought Asia was a desert."

"Only part of it. Anyway, that's how they drew them then."

Sandra stood on her toes and looked at the map closely.

"Look! They have a book in the middle of a country."

"That's not a country, it's a city. It's where my grandfather came from. They have palm trees there. And they don't have boogers in the orange juice."

Sandra looked at me. "Actually," she said quietly, "I know about that place. It's in the Bible."

"You're talking about a different Ninevah."

"No. I know from Sunday school. There was war there. They have a library. And now... now it's this place you can visit."

We stood there deadlocked. My mother called from the kitchen and asked did we want more tea.

"No," said Sandra, "I have to go."

When she left, I went to my mother in the kitchen and told her what Sandra Greenaway had told me about Ninevah. My mother was taking another braided bread out of the oven, and I thought it selfish that she hadn't offered any to us. She took out the bread and began to glaze it with green frosting. The frosting was dark, just like the green on the map. I told her it didn't look like the sort of thing people would want to eat.

"It's for Irma Burr," she said. Irma Burr lived upstairs and was Irish. "I'm making it for St. Patrick's day."

While my mother frosted the braided bread, I told her that Ninevah existed in the Bible and people like Sandra Greenaway got to learn about it in Sunday school. I told her Ninevah had a library.

My mother didn't answer. She put a towel around the bread and looked away. Then she put the bread on the plate and handed it to me.

"Now you bring this up to Irma Burr," she said, "and tell her *top o' the morning.*"

A HIDDEN CITY

As result of unspoken covenants children make, Sandra Greenaway and I never visited each other's houses again. Now, however, I took great care to study Ninevah on the map, and the more I looked, the more I decided that a real and vital city was right beneath it. I could see this city: outdoor markets with pomegranates, jewelry, enormous bolts of cloth, as well as dark blue bottles that certainly contained genies. I decided the map-maker had never been to Ninevah, but had drawn it from some idea he'd gotten from a book. I told this to my mother and she said I was talking nonsense.

Later I learned that Ninevah had once been considered a holy city. The library it housed was famous, and the city was named for a goddess called Eve who helped pregnant women use their own ribs to make their children's bones. But we never discussed any of these things in our house. It wasn't part of our life to dwell on this city by the Tigris.

II

THE JOURNEY OF THE MAP

When I was thirteen, instead of going to school, I spent long tedious hours in my parents' car, which was always parked in back of our apartment building. My father never left for the university until eleven, and I had to crouch low in the car, so he wouldn't see me from the window. It never occurred to me my father might go to the car, and he never did. His movements were always furtive, slow, careful not to wake my mother. I could see his wide moon face framed in the sun porch window. Mysterious rituals. Ablutions. My father was unobserved.

My father always did unremarkable things, like drink coffee, straighten up. Since we were both behind glass, I always imagined we were living in different elements. The things he did were remarkable only in that he didn't know I was seeing him, although I always imagined that he was going to do something outrageous. Once, when he picked up a piece of paper, I was sure it was the map, which my mother had put away. It wasn't, though. It was a plan of the cathedral of St. Gall. My father was studying it for a course he was teaching.

An hour after my father left for the university by bus, I snuck out of the alley, and took a different bus to downtown Lawrence. Two times a week, I saw a leering fifty-one-year-old

Spanish tutor who came close, very close, to ravishing me. If I was early, I rode endlessly, getting off at random stops. The air was pale, thin, attenuated. Time disappeared. Tenements rose like pieces of a stage set. Sometimes I read in the green marbled bathroom of Lawrence's best department store, sitting on a wrought iron chair just like the matrons. I was a fugitive. Anybody looking at me should know that. But all the matrons smiled at me: "*You look so pretty with your hair and all, dontcha know?*" This made me feel normal. I always smiled back.

From the department store's enormous windows, Lawrence spread before us like a gray prairie. While the matrons talked, I read important books: Freud, Dostoievsky, Faulkner. The women didn't know these books—they only spoke about my hair. After I left the department store and lay recklessly on a couch with the Spanish tutor, I came home and lied to my parents about school. I told them what I had learned in Spanish, how much volleyball I had played, and the next morning typed a note, excusing my absence, and stuck it in front of my mother's face. As always, she was asleep. She signed it without reading it.

The map had disappeared: I wondered if my mother had given it back to my grandfather, but when I asked her she said: "I'd never do a thing like that. It's an heirloom. I just got tired of it. You can look at things like that for so long." However, the day my father got a new teaching job in Vermont, my mother brought the map out and laid it on the dining room table.

"Old memories," she said, puffing at a cigarette. She pointed to the map. "Is this where you go when you don't go to school?"

"I always go to school. What do you think?"

"Whatever," said my mother. She smoked the cigarette and tapped ashes in the ashtray. The ashtray was glass and had an indentation where the cigarette was supposed to go, but my mother never put the cigarette there.

"We're going to Vermont," she said. "My father is very upset."

For a minute I didn't know which father she meant. It was

my father, after all, who'd gotten a new teaching job. Then I realized it was her father.

"My father," she continued, "liked visiting us here. It's different from New York. It gives him a break."

"Are you giving him the map?"

"Nonsense. It's an heirloom."

I looked closely at the map: What had once seemed verdant now looked poisonous. Purple and green ink. Who had thought to use those colors anyway? I was going to tell this to my mother, then thought the better of it.

"We're getting a big house, you know," she said. "Lots and lots of rooms."

"Yes, Mom, I know."

"So the map can go anywhere. Anybody who wants it can have it."

M Y FATHER'S STUDY

When we moved to Vermont, to a town that did not seem real, I discovered sleeping in the afternoon. In Kansas, I never had slept in the afternoon. In that flat, horizontal land, day was omnipresent. But Vermont gave the promise of eternal night. Its hills dipped and curved. Its houses had attics, window seats, sloping closets. And the town itself was in a valley, surrounded by green mountains.

School began earlier than school in Kansas. Also I was going to school now, not hiding in my father's car. I went to late-night pizza parties and found a boyfriend my own age. In the afternoons, I came home tired.

Before I slept, I always went to my father's study to do my homework. His study was in the basement, half below ground-level, with clerestory windows on two sides, eye-to-eye with rose bushes. There was a sense of order and secrecy in my father's room that didn't permeate the rest of the house, which was open, and sprawled like a log cabin. My father's papers were stacked and labeled like seedlings in a well-tended garden. The air was filled with the soft smell of dark ink and fresh paper. Above me I heard my mother and sister talking, often arguing. Without knowing it, I'd begun to regard them with contempt, and I dug deep into my books with a monk-like, masculine virtue. It was an accident that I was a woman, an unlucky one, I thought. I also loved men passionately. That was unlucky, too.

My father was now the overseer of the map's nomadic journey. He'd hung it above a couch in an alcove in his study. The alcove was built into a wall with no windows. This made it feel tucked away, like a trundle bed.

194

After I did my homework, I went over to the couch, pulled my coat over my legs, and fell asleep. Before I slept, I often looked at the map and imagined I was a traveler in a desert who was given refuge in a tiny village. I was on my way to deliver a dangerous message, something that might cost me my life; but for now I was lying in a white-washed room, listening to someone bustle in the kitchen. When I finally fell asleep it was always thick, nearly imageless, yet imbued with purpose, even speed, as I moved through some unknown country. I ignored towns, landmarks, anything that might stop me and when I woke up, I knew I'd been traveling. This feeling persisted when I went upstairs.

My father never worked in his study until evening. If he happened to come home early from the university and came downstairs, he didn't wake me, but turned on lights, pulled the shades, straightened the furniture, and once, just once, leaned over and kissed me on the cheek. I pretended to sleep—a remote and indifferent princess, my hair arrayed upon the pillow for my father.

My father hadn't always been easy to have as a father. He was punctilious, shy, and kind, except for a terrible temper that emerged without warning. When I was five, in a strange summer house, he pulled down my pants, held my legs up in the air and whipped me again and again. I didn't know why he was doing this and said, many times, as if to make sense of it, *You are whipping me.* This was the sort of thing that I had to watch out for.

One afternoon I woke up late. We were already in the deep brittle dark of a cold Vermont winter. The air was blue-black. A strange, ethereal consistency. And outside, next to the clerestories, were the boots and legs of a man I didn't know. The boots were kicking the earth, and I heard him say:

"She's not going to last the winter. You'll have to do something."

My father's voice answered but I couldn't hear what he was saying.

"No, she won't," said the man, as if he had been contradicted. "Mr. Hucksworth wouldn't listen to me when I told him. He said, 'I don't want the expense.'"

My father pointed out that whatever was in question had lasted for a long time.

"But she won't last now," said the man. "You can bet she won't." He kicked the ground again. They walked off, muttering.

I could guess they were talking about a water pipe—something that Mr. Hucksworth, the original builder of the house, hadn't installed properly. But I chose not to know. Instead, I decided, perversely, that they were talking in code—possibly about me, or my mother or my sister. I looked closely at the map—the woman spilling water, the words *Lector Benevol*. I fell asleep again and this time really dreamt that I was on a desert, going to a city like Ninevah, except that it was older and had no library. My mission was perilous, obscure. I traveled at night under unfamiliar stars. I looked for the town with the oasis and couldn't find it. *I have to keep going*, I thought to myself.

When I woke, there were familiar sounds upstairs—my mother and father arguing. It was about the pipes, after all: My mother wanted them replaced. My father didn't.

"We'll freeze," she said. "We'll freeze our goddamn asses off."

"We won't," he said. "We've never frozen in our lives."

It was usually the case that both of my parents were right. I believed this now, warm from my desert journey. I went upstairs and soon all of us were traveling. We argued about the water pipes and, when we got tired of that, about the state of the Soviet Union. We traveled full speed, courting unfamiliar gestures.

The Antique Writing Chest

The antique writing chest came from England and was the sort of chest gentlemen of means took on journeys in the 19th century. It had drawers, boxes for pen, ink, paper, sealing wax, and a tilted surface that one could write on. I'd bought the chest in England when I was seventeen, and my parents and I took a winding road to the Brontës' house. There we saw the impossibly small buttons on Charlotte's wedding dress, incomprehensible books the children had written in code—and the graveyard beyond their house. The antique store was at the bottom of the hill, and my mother, who noticed the writing chest, said that I should buy it.

"It's not my sort of thing, Mom," I said.

"Buy it," my mother said, who had forsaken maps for antiques. "You'll never regret it. It's marvelous."

I didn't want the chest. I wanted to be in seedy French hotels with shutters like Matisse paintings. I wanted to wake up with my boyfriend in a tangle of sheets and the smell of sour wine. Nonetheless, I bought the chest to please my mother and she found someone in Vermont to refinish it. Soon the mahogany shone and the brass handles were so bright they would have attracted highway robbers. I never liked the refinished chest, but kept it in my room as an oddity. Eventually, when I left home, my mother moved herself into my bedroom, which she always called "my writing room."

"The chest is there," she always said. "Are you sure that you don't want it?"

What I really wanted was the map, which I had come to love again, during hours of long imageless sleep in my father's study. "No, mother," I told her. "The chest should be at home."

III

A WALK IN THE SNOW

It is night, deep night, and I am walking up a steep hill to a house I haven't visited in more than twenty years. The driver has let me out at the bottom of the hill, just as he did twenty years ago when I used to take the bus from college. The hill is far too steep for the bus, and the driver, an old Vermont veteran, believes walking in the snow is good for people. As always, I am stricken by the belief the snow will swallow me up. As always, I am convinced our house has fallen into a precipice. Yet I find the house and walk up the steps, just as I did twenty years ago.

The last time I came home, walking up the same hill, I kept thinking of a particular phrase and I am thinking of it again: *here I come in all the fury of my consumption.* I long to tell the phrase to my father, just as I longed to tell it to him twenty years ago, and I want to ask him if he has ever heard it and then say how odd it is that I thought the very same thing the last time I came home. Instead, I sit opposite him at the mahogany dining room table drinking sherry and explaining how my husband and son are stuck in a broken-down rented car in Boston. Everything is the same except that my mother is dying.

My mother's death will not be a normal death. It will be ambiguous, wrenching, hard, just like her life. Indeed, the ambiguity looms so large the very thought *my mother is dying* makes me feel like a heretic.

"She isn't dying," my father says. "She's only refusing to eat. She went to the hospital for a harrowing operation, but now she's refusing food. It's all those years of ice-cream cones. You know how she would just keep those ice-cream cones stacked by the stove and make herself a few every night? Maybe she's gotten used to them."

"Yes," I say. From where I am sitting, I can see a huge box of them. They are stacked in a corner, near the kitchen. I can also see the map of Asia which has moved from my father's study to the mantel: there is the nude woman who used to embarrass me, the Christ-like figure offering a cup and saucer.

"Lector Benevol," I say, referring to the words on Ninevah.

"Of course," says my father. He knows Latin well.

I won't sleep in my parents' house, but will sleep at my brother's who lives in the same Vermont town. The fact that I won't sleep at home is a silent, unspoken code. Our family doesn't have to talk though we talk all the time.

"It must be a long time since you've seen snow," my father says while he drives through quiet white streets.

"I live in the colonies, now," I say, meaning California.

My brother lives on the edge of town. He lives in one half of a house, his girlfriend and her daughter in the other. It's hard to tell if they're having separate, enmeshed, or semi-detached lives and no one ever asks them. My father stops outside the house. It's a given that he won't go in.

E ATING

When I first see her in the hospital, my mother's breath is sickeningly sweet. She's surrounded by a mist of eerie perfume, shriveled beyond recognition. A crocheted bandage holds the wrist with the IV and this looks quaint and archaic, like a glove from Mother Goose. *She is a puzzle*, say the doctors. *A medical puzzle.*

I don't think my mother is a puzzle. I think she wants to die and no one is letting her. I think she's beset by the false jollity of the nurses. (*Marla! Are you hungry! Gotta eat your food to get strong!*) The denial of my uncle. (*Her color looks good.*) And the controlled calm of her Iranian psychiatrist with his almost-perfect English accent. (*Shock therapy, combined, of course, with other appropriate interventions... would, in my opinion....*)

While people speculate, I see my mother's dim, struggling presence. The rise and fall of her breath. Small moments of small recognition. Larger moments of self-disgust. (*I will start to eat tomorrow. Yes. I promise. But later. You better go.*)

I have presents for my mother: A small doll house I found at the airport. A silver box from Tibet containing messages from my husband, my son, and my daughter. I also have brought her a white shawl her own mother crocheted. She pushes everything away. "I have no use for these."

"The silver box is useless. You have to keep it."

Later she touches my hair, my eyes, looking for the flaw. "The nurses asked me what you did. I said you were an actress. They were impressed."

"Mother! I'm not an actress!"

"But you are! Don't you remember when you played Hamlet? You were marvelous opposite Ophelia. Tell me something. Are you wearing a bra?"

"Yes, mother, I'm wearing a sports bra. Look: the straps criss-cross in back. In the summer when you wear a lowcut dress, you can see these cool white straps."

This is the Zen of dying. The mystery of a criss-crossed bra. While I talk, my mother tries to breathe. Every breath is a struggle.

Meanwhile, in the next bed, a woman whose cancer has twisted around her lungs and esophagus like a snake is being visited by a handsome, dark-haired cleric in an impeccable wool suit. He is reading from a book about sin, and God taking bad lambs back into the fold. This woman does not look like a bad lamb. She looks like a gentle lamb. The cleric looks like a wolf who has never considered that death could happen to him because he has eaten so many lambs and gotten away with it. Perhaps it won't. He probably has his own opinions about Sauerkraut Day in this part of Vermont.

"...and the Lord returneth all to his flock..."

"Mother, listen. You know all the stuff we went through? The rough times? The hard times? It's all water under the bridge. All that matters is that I love you. Do you understand?" Blank look. Small, dim eyes. "Mother, I love you. It's been a long haul."

"Do you mean this?"

"Yes. "

"No you don't."

"I do."

I know my mother the way I know the air. I know her the way I know cats who come for an evening and then live on. I know her the way I know a garden in Kansas, over thirty years ago, brimming with lilacs and a rough stone birdbath.

Mother, do you want to die?

No.

Then why aren't you eating?

I can't.

You Have to Come to Me

You have to come to me, my mother said on the phone. *I am dying and you have to come to me.* In the small dormer room of my brother's house, I think that perhaps for all her oddities she has been a secret avatar, like those mad Tibetan deities with frightening masks and curlicues of smoke roiling from their auras. Or maybe she will die calmly, like the Zen Master Bassho, who knew the precise hour of his departure.

A Visit to Ninevah

"The question is, why now? Why isn't your mother eating now?"

It is New Year's Eve and I am talking to my mother's psychiatrist on the phone. It's eight o'clock in the evening and Ari Nafissian has called me at my brother's house. His voice is controlled, concerned: studied solicitude with a hint of the real.

"But I understand you want to transfer my mother to a place where she can get shock therapy...."

"Yes. It is a good idea for her." He speaks English softly and correctly and has cultivated the practice of pausing before speech.

"I understand. They say this place has good facilities. Tell me...what do you think it will do?"

"Well. Your mother isn't eating. It may get her started."

A pause between us. Of what? Understanding? I think of the children's rhyme: *How many miles to Babylon?*

"But what do you see as the benefit in my mother's eating?"

"Well, she'll start to eat again."

"I understand. But she's been depressed all her life. What will she go back to once she starts to eat? She can't enjoy food. She doesn't enjoy buying clothes. What will eating for a few months do for her?"

"Well, of course, we'll have to look for ongoing therapy after the shock treatment. And still appropriate drugs. But why has she stopped eating now? I mean a person can be depressed and want to stop living for three days, and then suddenly feel like living. Our job is to preserve life."

"This was for more than three days. More like four thousand. To put it differently, have you ever thought there's a shred of sanity in what my mother is doing?"

Our conversation is beginning to sound like a book on conversational English. *Which way to the hospital? Three turns after the light. Do they have any beds there? Oh yes. Care-worn and crafted well, in the style of the old country.*

"Excuse me," I say quietly. "But is there a shred of sense to what she's doing?"

Ari Nafissian pauses. For a moment we step into another realm; an erotic, almost sacred current flows between us.

"There was a legend about a nomad who fasted for that long," he says to me. "She went to the desert and became a healer."

"This nomad was a woman?"

"Yes. It's an old Assyrian legend. Maybe as old as Ninevah."

"And so?"

"And so I never give up hope."

I hear my brother in back of me. He's cooking something—rice with pine nuts, roasted peppers. He's cooking in a way that tells me he doesn't want to hear the conversation.

"Well, it's beyond the call of duty to talk on New Year's Eve," I say. "So there's only more question, and you don't have to answer it."

"Oh no," he says. "Please ask."

"Well if this were your grandmother. I mean, if this were *your* 74-year-old grandmother, living in Iran, who'd been depressed for years and had very little to live for—is shock-treatment what you would want for her if she stopped eating?"

Long pause. Unhappy silence. "Yes. I would recommend it."

THE POST BOX

Before I leave, my father gives me the antique writing chest—a burden to take home on the plane. When I get home, I open it idly, expecting to find nothing. Instead I find all my mother's writing: letters she has started—often to me—and never finished, notes that toy with suicide, five or six journal entries so close to my sense of her, I'm not sure if they're hers or mine.

The dreamer sleeps and nothing can stop her, she wrote, *because sleep is a consuming passion, a lust that no one can observe. At the same time sleep, the domain of the sleeper, is not comforting. It is cold, solid, burdensome. The eyelid repairs the night. It is morning and the typical day is commenced. Only the seasons change....*

There are also other things in the chest: birthday candle-holders from years ago, letters from me, a picture of my mother when she was thirteen, an improbable braided candle—the kind that's used to light candles on the Sabbath. There is also a single sentence, written on yellow note paper and it looks quite recent: *When Eurydice knew she was to be chosen she suddenly became afraid even though it was really a very elaborate sojourn that was being prepared for her.... There was nothing to go by, not even a map....*

I look at everything. The plastic candle-holders in the shape of birds. A wooden rattle I played with when I was three. And it occurs to me my mother knew I would find everything in the chest. Who would have guessed, when we found it in England, that it would become a haphazard postal system between a mother and a daughter?

The chest smells like my mother: the smell of Ponds Cold Cream—unguents of the fifties and sixties. I put the chest in the living room. It stays there like a heartbeat.

IV

THE MAGICIAN'S EYE

After we left Vermont, my husband flew back to California to be with our six-year-old-daughter, and my son and I went to New York, the city of my mother's childhood. It was a chilling winter, the kind where your tongue sticks to ice and your breath precedes you everywhere. Yet compared to California, the contrast between the indoors and the outdoors made us both feel safe. We relished the sense of walls, snow and sky. We took comfort in boundaries close to our skin, cold that was bracing, warmth that could be retrieved.

My son, who was almost eleven, was angry at me for taking him to see my mother. He hadn't liked the presence of death. He hadn't liked seeing someone starve. One night he did karate kicks in the hotel room until he succeeded in turning off the light switch with his foot.

"Why did you take me there?" he asked. "I didn't like the way she smelled."

"Because it was the right thing to do," I said. "And tomorrow we're going to Ellis Island."

"Why?"

"Because you might find out something there."

"Like what?"

"Like what your grandmother's parents did in order to come here."

It was bitter cold on the ferry to Ellis Island. Everyone was dressed in layers, like immigrants, except for my son. I cried when we entered the Registry Hall: This was a real passage in my grandfather's journey, before he became a mapmaker, a doctor, a lecher. He had been frightened, bewildered—and amazed that he'd taught himself English on the boat. "I astounded them," he told me once. "I wrote a compound sentence in English!"

The Registry Hall was perfectly, monastically, empty. I wandered among exhibits. My son sat alone like a monk in a large cathedral. His face was lit by sun from the enormous domed windows and he read a book called *The Magician's Eye*. I imagined my grandfather watching his only grandson read the language he'd taught himself on the ship. I imagined my grandfather weeping.

On the ferry going back to Manhattan, my son said he hadn't liked Ellis Island at all.

"Angel Island's better," he said, referring to the place where immigrants in California were processed. "Here they tried to make it look pretty. At Angel Island they *showed* you the wretched conditions."

My son talked so loudly, a man in a yarmulke smiled at me, and I realized I felt bereft. Back in the hotel, my son did more karate kicks.

"Why did you take me to that stupid island?" he said.

"It wasn't a stupid island," I said. "And tomorrow we're going to the Lower East Side so you can see how your relatives really lived."

We didn't go to the Lower East Side after all. Instead, we walked through Greenwich Village where I bought my son a box decorated with a single eye. This eye reminded him of the third eye that belonged to the magician in the book he read in the Registry Hall and he pronounced it "way cool." Afterwards, we went to Washington Square Park, where my son slid down an artificial ice hill again and again. Each time he did, he cried with delight—as though he could reinvent his past in that formidable cold.

THE TIBETAN BOOK OF THE DEAD

My mother outsmarted everybody by dying an hour after a well-intentioned nurses' aide painted her nails pink. There was no funeral—she hadn't wanted one—and since Vermont has strict codes about the time lapse between death and embalming, I never saw her again. My father told me her face had a curious dignity in death. I told him she had done the right thing.

For a long time I couldn't believe my mother had died. It was not like missing her. We'd rarely been able to talk. It was more disbelief at the sudden absence of something in nature, as though an enormous gorge had been swallowed up, or the moon was no longer in the sky. To offer some kind of homage I decided to read to my mother from *The Tibetan Book of the Dead*. This wasn't the first time I'd done this for my atheist, Marxist relatives. Perhaps it was a compensation for never being what they wanted me to be:

Mother. This mind of yours is inseparable luminosity and emptiness in the form of a great mass of light. It will guide you through the bardo. Mother. You are becoming one with the white light.

"My mom is being weird," my son said audibly from the kitchen. He and his friend were making snacks. "She's reading from a book like my grandmother can hear."

"Yeah," the friend said. "Well moms are into weirdness."

That night at dinner my husband made a cruel joke:

"Your mother's reading from The Tibetan Book of the Deaf," he said to our son and daughter.

"What?" they asked, glad to get real information.

"This is what it is," said my husband cupping his hands. "'GO TOWARD THE WHITE LIGHT!' 'What?' 'I SAID GO TOWARD THE WHITE LIGHT.'"

The children laughed. I didn't. By now it was the 49th day of my mother's death, and, according to Tibetan calculations, she was preparing to be reborn. I couldn't imagine my mother doing such a thing. All I could imagine was how she would be ordering fabrics for a new and interesting living room. Once again I opened the book. *Please choose a loving home,* I said to her.

MILDRED

After my mother died, I was no longer able to write because I realized it had been her, after all, that I'd been writing to all along. My mother had not liked my writing, and was disappointed that I didn't write like H. H. Munro or Henry James or any one of a number of people who wrote in what she called good simple ways. "Why don't you write what you know about?" she often asked.

It was only when she died that I realized my mother was a confining wall, one I must scale again and again every time I wrote. I lived in California, she in Vermont and sometimes I'd think of her at home, three hours later because of the time difference, and imagine what she was doing. I wondered whether she was eating (usually ice cream cones), or whether she was watching television (most probably she was). I had deep regrets about her sense of emptiness, and the antique writing chest didn't help them, because I knew the emptiness she felt wasn't the emptiness mystics talk about, but an illusory emptiness that comes when one can't use one's powers.

I asked my father for the map of Asia and put it all on a wall near the antique writing chest, thinking I'd invent a story about Ninevah. A day later, though, I took it down and put it in my closet. It was my mother's story, not mine—about what the mapmaker might have done on the deserts of Ninevah—and every time I looked at it, all I could think of was that the story was there, hidden in the folds of the map, the way, at night, when I looked up from my desk, I imagined there was a cosmic lining in the sky, and if only I could rip it open, everything that was to be known would tumble out. My husband didn't notice that I'd taken down the map. We had reached a stage of apathy that went far beyond paying attention.

During that time, however, a curious kind of help came, and this was in the form of a pale woman, who looked almost exactly like my mother would have looked had she been happy. She was a small woman in her seventies with a hooked nose, and tiny, fluttering arms. She wasn't enrolled in the writing program I taught in, but sat in the back of the room, a grateful wraithlike radiance. I could tell that her only pleasure in life was to be allowed to audit a writing class. I told her she could stay.

My mother had always wanted to be a writer and might have been a good one. But she wasn't able to withstand the occupational hazards of the trade nor did she have an audacious belief in the powers of her imagination. Her favorite line was from the *Cherry Orchard*, in which a character whose name eluded her said, "I could have been a Dostoievski."

This woman, whose name was Mildred, sat in the back of the room, or, on days when she was bold, in a corner, quite close to me. She had a mole at the end of her nose, and until I looked closely I could never tell whether this mole was skin or moisture. This added to the impression that Mildred was melting. She always wore a green sweater covered with small wooden balls and dark brown pants. She had glasses like my mother's, but her eyes emanated light. As I fielded competitive remarks from other students, all I saw in her was a beatitude. *I have been blessed*, I thought, *like a character in a story about Hassidim. My mother has returned to let me teach her.*

I was embarrassed by my belief that Mildred had been sent to me. I was embarrassed, too, that I took to writing paeans to her that I never showed to anybody. I wrote them longhand in a sort of hieroglyph that even I wasn't meant to decipher, and although I've never tried to translate my handwriting, they were the first things I wrote after my mother died. When a mean-spirited student asked why I was letting a seventy-year-old woman who wasn't in my writing program audit a class that qualified graduate students hadn't been able to get into, I looked at these very notes and said Mildred had once been an accomplished teacher and I wanted her to critique me. The student didn't believe me, but when she complained, the head of the department looked the other way. Perhaps Mildred had been his lover once. Or maybe he knew I was reeling from my mother's death. The idea of the two of them in bed amused me. She was so frail, he could break her bones.

Mildred gave me just one story. It was about an older woman who took a younger woman in as a boarder in her cavernous apartment. The younger woman, who was a cellist, spent hours playing Bach Inventions while the older woman served her tea. She met an archaeologist and left to get married.

I found the story lovely—generous, well-written and understanding in a way my mother had never understood me. I waited for Mildred to come back so I could tell her how much I liked it, but she'd vanished. Later I discovered she'd gone to many classes in the writing program, always submitting the same story. "No doubt she wrote it herself, but a long time ago," a colleague said. Then she laughed a short bitter laugh. I asked her what the story was about. The colleague said it was about buying a rug in a peasant town in Italy. This convinced me that Mildred had written about the cellist for me alone. I continue to believe that she was sent. I continue to believe that my mother allowed me to teach her.

A SHES

My father, who did not believe in funerals, could not bury my mother's ashes. He kept the box that contained them in a closet, and after the last guest went away and the last dish was washed, he sometimes went to the closet and stood close to them. On top of this box he'd put my mother's ring, which the funeral parlor wrapped in a black velvet bag. He also put the miniature oval silver box from Tibet I'd given my mother when I visited her in the hospital. The silver box was used for prayers, and contained the written message *dear mother, we send you all our love and here is a mantra which means I am the jewel in the center of the lotus, mother remember, you are also the jewel in the center of the lotus, love, cecelia, nicholas, justin and tanya.*

My daughter Tanya was only six and it was hard for her to write in the small cramped space, but she'd done it anyway. My father thought all religions were bunk, yet once told me that when he looked inside and saw the miniature message, he had an odd sense that all four of us were looking up and waving at him.

"The oddest thing," he said to me. "The oddest goddamn thing."

We lived three thousand miles away, so my father told me about the ashes over the phone. "It's very comforting, although it bothers me a little, like being close to a shrine. Sometimes I even want to talk to her."

About the ashes, I had conflicted feelings, which is often the case with me. On the one hand, I thought my father should bury my mother. On the other, I thought it was good that this scholarly man, who didn't believe in shrines, should do something that made sense to him.

"Please, Dad," I said. "Do whatever you need to do. It's been a terrible time. "

One day my father came to California to see me, and brought me some of my mother's ashes, as well as a white shawl she'd liked. The shawl, like the antique writing chest, smelled of Ponds Cold Cream, and also Eau de Vie perfume, which used to make me nauseous when I was trapped in a car with her. I buried my face in her shawl, sickened and moved simultaneously. I opened the ashes, which were wrapped many times over in a plastic bag: They were rough, sandy and contained one dark metal circle—part of my mother's artificial hip. It looked like an ancient coin.

"Where's that map of Asia?" my father asked.

"It made me sad, so I put it away."

"I want it," said my son boldly. "I want it for my own room." He was angry that I hadn't given him the map, as well as the writing chest. He loved old things and was especially drawn to the map.

"Someday," I told him. "It's not the time."

My father and I stood silently, acknowledging what we didn't want to acknowledge: that objects which meant so much to my mother were now in our own ambivalent archives. I said I'd hang the map on the mantle as soon as I stopped being sad. Both of us knew I never would.

In truth, I wanted to bury my mother in Ninevah. I wanted to visit the ruined city myself, and also wanted her to be close to Eve, the Goddess of the Rib, who helped pregnant women make their children's bones. I wanted her to wander in the library there, look at fabrics in the open market place. I wanted her to feel the lush verdant green of that ancient Assyrian city.

My mother, however, had always wanted to be buried in the poets' corner of Westminster Abbey, so finally, on a short trip to England, I took my portion of her ashes there. Since Westminster is heavily-guarded, and I'm an extremely cautious person, I pretended to be looking at Elizabeth Barrett Browning's grave, all the while putting my hands in my pockets, retrieving dust, and touching the stone lovingly. Soon the grave was covered with a rough gray ash. My mother's ash. My mother bones. I kept the coin-shaped object in the writing chest.

One day my father asked whether I might consider putting my portion of my mother's ashes underneath the stone Buddha in our backyard. I hadn't known he'd seen this Buddha and couldn't tell him the ashes were long gone—picked up by sturdy shoes in England, taken down London streets, dusted off on British carpets. I suddenly felt mean-spirited and said I'd think about it, in return for my mother's wedding ring which she once said she wanted me to have. My father said a decent daughter would never barter for her mother's resting place. I reminded him my mother often liked to barter—was sometimes better at bartering than living.

THE MAP

The map is still in my closet, close to where I kept my mother's ashes. Sometimes I take it out and travel miles, knowing I won't put it up in my house again. This map is nomadic like the Torah, and has done its job with my mother and her family: instead of treks on the desert, or days in hiding with a rabbi, it goes from house to house, room to room, neither an heirloom, nor something that can be given away. At some point the map will belong to my son: since he never met the map-maker or heard my mother's stories, he'll treat it with more dispassion than I ever did. He'll probably create the map again and Ninevah will become a bustling modern city, close to its home on the Tigris, a green and mysterious accident.

Printed September 1997 in Santa Barbara
& Ann Arbor for the Black Sparrow Press by
Mackintosh Typography & Edwards Brothers Inc.
Text set in Goudy Old Style by Words Worth.
Design by Barbara Martin.
This first edition is published in paper wrappers;
there are 200 hardcover trade copies;
100 hardcover copies have been numbered &
signed by the author; & 20 copies lettered
A-T have been hardbound in boards by
Earle Gray & signed by the author.

Photo: Jane Scherr

THAISA FRANK was born in the Bronx, and has lived in Manhattan, California, Illinois, France, and Ohio, where she got a degree in philosophy from Oberlin College. She has also studied linguistics and philosophy at Columbia University. Her stories have been anthologized and won PEN awards. She is the author of *Desire* (Kelsey Street Press, 1982), a collection of short fiction, and *A Brief History of Camouflage* (Black Sparrow Press, 1992), a collection of short fiction and a novella. She has taught creative writing at San Francisco State, UC Berkeley, UC Berkeley Extension, and various summer writing programs, including the Naropa Institute in Boulder, Colorado. As a Contributing Editor to the *San Francisco Review* she has written extensively about the writing process, and is co-author of *Finding Your Writer's Voice* (St. Martin's Press, 1994). Currently she teaches at the University of San Francisco, is co-host of the Writers Conference on the WELL and lives in Oakland with her son, Casey Rodarmor. In addition to teaching, she has a private practice as a psychotherapist and writing consultant.